LIGHT SPEED

PARCHED
BOOK SIX

Z.L. ARKADIE

FLAMING
HEARTS

CHAPTER 1

THE CALL

ADORE

I am with my mother, Ce'lah'ime, gathering fruit for the Tilt. I love watching her skin glow. She's the shade of the puek leaf, shimmering like gold and diamonds under the eternal sun. We've come to the Forest of Naught to pick the ci'ke, ton'rek, and ci'cha fruit. *Duk*, three. That is how many fruits are needed for celebrating the eastward leaning of the perpetual sun.

My mother insisted on the ci'ke, ton'rek, and ci'cha. I wanted the lu'kek, pin'kek, and ze'ru, but she said it was necessary for me to acquire a taste for the fruit that grows in the Forest of Naught. When I asked her why, she offered no reason.

"Ve'ku, nek, Tet'ram'kek, Ce'lah'ime," I say to her, pleading one last time.

"Speak English, Adore," she gently scolds.

"Please, can we go to the Forest of Whispers?" I say as we stop at the sprawling, purple-leaved vekt bush where the ci'ke grows. "It's better there."

Ce'lah'ime's mouth stretches into a smile, and she touches my cheek. She is a gentle mank'et, the creature who is able to give suck when her belly is full with child, like the human woman. She is the only mank'et ever to distend at the belly and breasts, giving birth to the seven daughters of Felix Benel.

"My Ad'ru..." There is sadness in her bright scarlet eyes. "We'll take these. You will like them. You'll see."

"Yes," I humbly acquiesce while reaching to pull a ci'ke off its spiky branch.

I choose to complain no more. Instead, I relish in the eastward sun. Its delicate rays glide across my skin, and I feel as if I'm being kissed on the lips a million times by Tryst. He's in the Forest of Whispers, gathering with Links and Valor. I always miss him when we are apart, but never in the way Cl'auta longs for the Selell Ze Feldis, or Na'ta for the Selell Telman.

Yet Tryst's nearness does make my insides tickle. The feeling is like sliding down Jaf'ra Falls when the waters transform from gray to green. That's when the current is the fastest. But that's the only effect he has on me. He doesn't make my thighs burn or head grow light and giddy. I have felt those sensations in my sisters when they are around their Selell bonds. That such a thing can happen to me is terrifying. I hope it never does.

The thought of bonding with a Selell troubles me as I fill my basket with the dark purple ci'ke. Each fruit is ripe for the picking. Ce'lah'ime, who usually hums a hymn of gratitude to the trees whenever she picks from them, is silent. I detect a kernel of sadness in her eyes, and I notice that she scarcely looks at me.

"Mother," I begin excitedly, attempting to brighten her mood.

Now she smiles, and I already feel relieved.

"After the feast, Tryst, Bohem, and I are going to the Vast Sea to chase the sickels," I announce with unconstrained jubilance.

We, I, can hardly wait. The sickels of the Vast Sea are quicker than the average ones. They are elusive and enjoy being pursued in the watery depths. If you can keep up, then you'll be rewarded. They will lead you to uncharted territory. Once they brought us to a huge dome with walls made of solid emerald; that's what we call it—te'ko'lok be'kt, the emerald dome. The green waters stream in all directions along the slippery walls, and if you catch the right current, they will slide you across the wall, or up it, or in loops, or send you crisscrossing in so many directions. It's always surprising when it carries us in ways we never expected.

I am sure I look happy about my plans, and usually my expression is reflected in Ce'lah'ime's face—but not this time. Her dim smile curls downward at the corners.

"Mother, what is it?" I'm concerned, but not for her. Strangely, I'm only worried for myself.

She stares at my wide and curious expression. Her lips part slightly. She wants to speak, but she doesn't.

"Please," I beg.

After a moment, the smile I'm used to returns. "This is enough ci'ke, Ad'ru. Let's gather the ton'rek."

I walk behind her, following her to the trees which yield the fuzzy orange ton'rek. Our feet crunch in the grass, and the tender, warm wind presses against our skin.

"Tapeetha has left Enu?" she asks.

Her question takes me by surprise. "Yes." I don't want to speak of it.

The truth is, I am the only daughter of Felix Benel left in Enu. For that reason, I did not want to lead Cl'auta and the Selell Ze Feldis to Pan'a'tua. My entire heart had hoped that Pan'a'tua would resist them and stay in Enu, but she did not stay. And now...

"And Clarity and Ze Feldis have taken her to Earth?" my mother asks.

"Yes." I don't like her questions. I don't want to talk about it. Instead, I want to tell her more about the emerald dome and Tryst. "Who told you this?" My tone is sharp, but only because I sense the implications in her questions. My sisters are gone. I'm here. She must know, as long as I have a choice, I will never leave. I cannot live without her or Tryst or my home, my majestic Enu.

"Your father," she answers, just as I thought.

"But not for long, I'm sure," I sing with forced enthusiasm. "Maybe Na'ta will return for the Tilt. She loves the celebration. Not even I can do the Dance of Flows like she can." For some strange reason, I search over my shoulder and mutter, "I'm sure she'll show up." I am not certain.

My mother does not comment. Even she knows

that my hopes will be thwarted. I continue to follow her toward the ton'rek trees. We are engulfed by their fragrant mist.

She whips her face toward the Diamond Mountains to the north. "Ah," she sings with delight, "Felix Benel has arrived."

I feel as though I'm shrinking into my feet. This is all too strange. Even as I reach out to take in the energy of Enu, I cannot soothe my anxiety. He knows that I am the last of his daughters to leave Enu. What news will he bring me? I close my eyes to let the dread pass through me. My mother's warm hand touches my arm, and I open my eyes.

"You gather the ton'rek, Ad'ru. I will join him," she says.

"You're leaving?" I ask, disappointed.

She puts her scarlet eyes on me. They are glassy, the closest she has ever come to crying. Enuians do not cry. Ce'lah'ime touches my face again then kisses the tip of my nose. She does this every time we part company, but this time, her lips linger longer than usual. What's frightening is that I feel nothing from her, none of the deep happiness usually contained within her. It can only be because she is *not* happy, and there's no reason for that. I'm here with her, she's gathering fruit for the Tilt, and my father, Felix, will soon join us. Why is she not happy?

She reaches into her basket to give me a ci'ke. "My gift upon parting."

In my mind, the tiny fruit seems to expand in her hand. It looks too heavy to bear.

"I don't understand, Ce'lah'ime…" I don't reach for it. I don't want to take the gift, although it's bad form not to accept it. I want her to withdraw the offer.

"Take it," she insists.

"But…" I hesitantly put my hand on the ci'ke.

After a moment of reading my face, she says, "You don't want it, Ad'ru?"

I shake my head, relieved she asked.

"Well then…" She puts the fruit back into her basket and surprises me by handing over the whole basket. "Then hold this while I answer your father's call."

My hand creeps up to latch onto the handle. Oh, how I wish she wasn't doing this. I can refuse her, although it would be a slight akin to striking her with my hand. So reluctantly, I take the basket and am left holding hers and mine too. A true smile has returned to her face. The happiness from within her emanates. My human heart expands with love, and my angst flutters away.

"Be Oh, Ad'ru," she says and kisses me once on my lips.

This makes me nervous again. She's given me the kiss of long journeys. I wonder if she's going away with my father. Will she not attend the Tilt? Yes! That has to be it. That is why she's given me her gatherings and is leaving so abruptly. Felix and Ce'lah'ime are bonded by something deeper than mere love. My mother told me how they came to be.

To the Enuians, when Felix was born, he was a novelty. They had never seen an infant, and so they came from every space on the orb just to get a glimpse and a whiff of him. He was nurtured by Meni'he, the tiller in the east spectrum, for the first eight years of his human life. That was when he first saw Ce'lah'ime. He was just a child, but she was not.

As soon as he could walk, he roamed the landscapes of Enu. Three years into his human age, he would climb the grassy mountain of Bar'-tuk'me whenever the sun tilted *dut*, or two degrees, west. That was when she appeared. *Tek te're'tu mank'et*. The Golden Lady. Those were the first words he ever spoke. For five years, at the same time of each long Enuian day, he hiked up the hill to watch the Golden Lady dive off the steep cliff into the crystal stream that ran along the ridge below.

At the end of his eighth year, Loel, the celestial guardian from the Higher Heavens, carried him away from Enu to rear him in the ways of the earth. Loel taught Felix human logic, science, languages, customs, and all about the power of his mind. My mother said it was during those years that my father saw and experienced the worst of mankind and, at times, the best. She says the worst is the reason he had very little joy.

He was twenty-six in human years when he returned to Enu as a curious mathematician and astronomer. And just as when he was a child, the Enuians journeyed from all parts of the orb to welcome the half celestial-half human being back to their world. With each kiss on the lips to mark his journey home—and there were thousands of them —he began to feel joy once again. The spirits of pure-hearted creatures, the perpetual daylight, and then the Golden Lady. Throughout the years, he'd never forgotten the way she leapt off the cliff, soaring through the air with her arms wide, legs piked behind her, as graceful as a willow leaf rides a burst of wind.

He thought he would have to wait until the sun tilted dut west to rest his yearning eyes upon the mank'et he had never forgotten. He even looked for her among the faces of those who had come to welcome him back to the land from where he came. However, he did not have to wait until dut west to see her. His humanity had set the mank'et creatures burning with lust for him, for the magnetism of his physical form and severe beauty, the brutish yet sweet smell of his human flesh and angelic composition. He was made from the heavens, and that reflected in his appeal.

On the day Ce'lah'ime ventured east to find Felix Benel, the son of the human and the angel, she found him pruning the bo'vek'et bushes, preparing them for the season of ripening. When he caught first sight of her, something amazing happened: her chest grew, giving her rounded breasts and nipples for suckling. With one look, he had chosen her as a mate, and from that moment on, they were bonded.

They are still special to each other. Humans call such a connection "married." If my father had it his way, he would never don the attire and occupation of a man and walk the earth again. He would remain home with his Ce'lah'ime and spend eternity here.

"Be oh," I say, beaming because now I know why she's behaving in such a manner. She's going to spend special time with my father and will miss the celebration of the Tilt!

"Good-bye," she whispers, and there it is again —the sorrow. But she is gone before I can question her about it.

I'm alone in the Forest of Naught. Other than Ce'lah'ime, Enuians do not venture here, even to gather the ci'ke, ton'rek, and ci'cha. I decide to gather a few more ton'rek and then rush off to join Tryst in the Forest of Whispers.

"Ad'ru," my father whispers.

Caught off guard, I call, "Father?"

"Ad'ru, come," he says.

I search ahead, toward the high regions where the ci'cha grow. There shines a light to one of the doorways fashioned by my father's power. My feet turn heavy. My intuition forbids me to go. This visit is unexpected. Father has already called for Ce'lah'ime. What does he want with me?

"Ad'ru," my father calls again.

Hearing his voice a second time makes me hurry forward to the door. "Father?"

I go stiff because something foreign grips me. I feel as if a hand has reached inside my chest and taken hold of my heart, and is squeezing the life out of it. In my entire existence, I have not sensed such terror. Is my father in distress? He has human parts. He once returned from the earth injured. However, he is able to heal himself.

"Run!" my instincts scream.

"Ad'ru, come now!" he demands.

His tone triggers movement in my feet. Although I'm gripped by fear and dread, I charge through the doorway, and I'm instantly swept up by a strange force. I can't see it, but I feel its presence. It's twisting my legs and my torso; it's bending my body forward and backward. It's so unrelenting that it takes no mercy on me when hard particles of some sort slam into my face, back, chest, and legs. This is chaos!

I choose to struggle to regain control of my limbs, but there's no winning. All I can do is give in to my aggressor's will. I squeeze my eyes shut to endure the attack and wait for it all to stop. A small number of seconds feel like forever, but finally the experience is over.

The noise. It's like zenet'tuk'ra, a million voices. And what's this sensation that's smothering me? Where's the warmth? What's squeezing the life out of me is bitter and prickly, scratching deep into my skin. I think—and I'm sure—that for the first time in my existence, I am cold.

My body is shivering. This is all too much to bear. My eyes are still shut tightly because I'm too afraid to open them and see what's around me. Slowly I open one eye and then the other. What I see causes a gasp to escape from my throat. Where is my sapphire sky that cuddles the perpetual sun that's tilted dut west? I'm trapped beneath a domed sky that's a swirl of white and gray. Are these human beings gazing down upon me?

"Are you all right, ma'am?" one shouts.

"Is she breathing?"

"Her eyes are open!"

"Is she alone?"

"Anyone with her?"

Their bodies range in size from husky to narrow, and their skins are the hues of the earth, like my sisters' and mine. Their brown and blue eyes are ablaze. I sense their fear and concern in equal parts. Only now do I realize that I'm gagging, choked by rank air.

"Somebody call 911!"

My eyes want to close, but I refuse to let them. My throat doesn't want to let this foul air into my body. I have to get home, back to Enu. It's hazy, but far off I see a white-stone temple with a steepled rooftop. All I have to do is lift myself off the cold, hard ground and fly toward it. There I will wait until my father comes to save me.

The edifices around me are tall and imposing. I reach toward them, intending to fly to them and hold on until my father comes to save me. But then I hesitate and consider the crowd's collective gasp. Through the haze, I see that, one by one, the humans are gazing at the newly blackened sky. The atmosphere grows colder. I'm no longer the only one who's deathly afraid.

Now more than before, I have to get far away. The humans only pay me scant attention as I gag and choke while attempting to lift myself off the concrete. I'm too weak to move my heavy limbs. Tears well up in my eyes, and a thick lump forms in my throat. This debilitating feeling makes me want to cry. Never in my life have I been so hindered.

"Cl'auta," I whimper. If this is Earth, then she's here. She has to come and save me.

To my relief, as my eyelids grow heavier, I see

beauty again. But he's not Cl'auta. *He's* delicate. His eyes are onyx, and his lips are ruby, and his white mane glistens in the sudden nighttime.

"She's with me," he shouts, but not loudly. His voice glides over me like the tepid dew that lays over the Meadow of Showers.

I use all my unspent energy to give him my hand. When he latches onto it, I quickly pull away from him. It's my worst fears realized. He is a Selell. He's going to kill me.

"Help," I whimper, but it's too late.

CHAPTER 2
THE BOND
ADORE

I'm conscious, although my eyes are still closed. I'm lying on a fluffy bed. Was I asleep? Had I fainted? I'm not sure. I've never been unconscious or asleep. My head feels as though it may soon explode, and my life center craves the lu'kek and pin'kek fruits.

I open my eyes slowly. I'm surrounded by four walls, and there's a huge, colorful stained-glass window to my left. The dark night sits behind it, but the dim light from the chandelier above this bed wakens the many colors in the glass. I remember the face of the Selell, his white hair, and his black eyes glaring down upon me. My hands fly up to rub both sides of my neck. I have not been bitten, and it seems as though I am still alive.

Beyond the doorway, I see a hallway lit with the same kind of artificial light the chandelier above the bed emits. I am worried about what or who roams beyond the threshold, but my stomach is pained by hunger. I have never in my life had such desire to eat.

Cl'auta, can you hear me? I cry, reaching out to her from deep within. I cannot feel her presence or hear her voice. I sense that a deliberate barrier had been set up to block me from reaching her.

Motivated by my hunger, I poke my head into the hollow hallway and call, "Oh, ek'k'ka!" *Greetings, my friend.*

I stand still, waiting for a response. I cannot believe I called a Selell my friend. If he is not of the Pact of Gogulon, then he is not a friend—he is a foe. Only silence returns my call. However, the cold that pains me is soothed by a warm mist that trickles down from above. I sigh with relief. This is the first inviting sensation I've felt since arriving to this place called Earth. And because of it, I easily step out of the confines of this room and into the hallway.

I reach a staircase and test my buoyancy by leaping over the banister. My feet hit the ground. I look up at where I last stood. Strange—my speed is hindered in this realm.

A sweet scent permeates this room with its regal, red velvet furnishings. I inhale, and the smell transports me across another threshold, down another short hallway, and into a place I recognize as a kitchen.

I see the baskets of fruit Ce'lah'ime on the counter. I hurry to swipe a ci'ke off the top of the batch and bite into the sweet purple flesh as though my life depends on it. I chew and bite, finishing one fruit and then another. My stomach is full by the fourth ci'ke. The pain in my head leaves, and I am again energized.

Ad'ru, in here… a voice I've once heard whispers between my ears.

After the initial jolt of fear passes, I reach out to touch the world around me. Another life force is near, although its energy confuses me. I gaze in the direction from which it calls. The i'lek'u is ignited within me as I tiptoe toward his voice.

There is another hallway. It's shorter, and a cold draft from the outside is trapped within its walls. The way out is near, which is confirmed when I reach a tall, wide, rustic wooden door. If there was ever a time to escape and find my way back home, it is now. I grab the doorknob and squeeze it tightly, but I'm consumed by terror. It's nighttime on Earth. Selells thrive in the darkness. Also, the air is cold outside, and I can barely tolerate it. Yet I feel that my chances of connecting with my sisters are greatly diminished from within the confines of this place. All will be well once I reach Cl'auta, who will then use the power of the mind to lead me to The House of Benel, where I will be safe.

I decide to leave, to run away from this creepy manor as fast as my body will carry me. But when I twist the doorknob, nothing happens. I try it again —nothing.

It dawns on me that I might be locked inside. So I kick the door with my bare feet and pound upon it with my palm. All I can hear is my own banging and knocking—my efforts are feverish but futile. It's a losing battle, but I won't stop, can't stop. Until…

"Ad'ru," the male calmly says from behind me.

I twist around and push my back tightly against the door. My heart is knocking so hard that even as I stand here with my eyes glued to the ominous creature, I feel the vibration in my throat. It's him, the creature with long white hair and black eyes. *The Selell.*

"Who are you?" I wheeze.

I wait for him to answer, but instead, he stares at me with such intensity that my insides tickle. My head goes so light that it feels as if it's floating above my shoulders. I am sorely confused, unable to figure out why gazing upon him makes me feel this way. A part of me wants to escape and find my sisters, but I want to stay too, only to be near him. He watches me with furrowed brows. He looks conflicted. So I toss the i'lek'u out of my palm to subdue him.

"No!" he roars, aiming his own palm at me.

I gasp. The light slams into his hand and returns to me.

"How did you do that?" I say breathlessly.

Still, he refuses to speak. There's no difference in his expression. What an odd creature, this Selell. I can't take my eyes off his sweater. It's a human's garment, and I've never seen anything look so attractive on a creature. It's black. His skin and hair are white. The way the neckline dips into a V-shape makes the contrast between his skin and the garment more remarkable. I want to touch this being who's having a peculiar effect on me, but I can't—because he is evil. I know this because he refused the light.

"Did you call my name?" I ask even though he hasn't answered anything I've asked him so far.

"I did," he mutters.

It's remarkable; he hasn't relaxed his frown as of yet.

"Did you deceive me in the Forest of Naught?"

He flinches and lifts one side of his mouth into a tiny bit of a smile. "No," he says in a lackluster tone.

I don't believe him. "You called me Ad'ru? That is my Enuian name." I push myself closer against the door and ready my palms in case a battle ensues. This time he will not be able to thwart my attack. "Are you ek'et'ru?"

"Ek'et'ru?" He frowns, confused.

"Evil incarnate."

There's a glow of amusement in his eyes, which have turned opaquely green. "No, I am not that." He's grinning but in a very strange manner. One side of his mouth is lifted higher than the other. There are intentions beyond goodwill behind it.

"You are a Selell?" I ask.

"Yes."

"And you know I have the lifeblood?"

"Yes." He's studying the rise and fall of my chest and possibly how my breaths slip out from between my lips.

"You don't want to kill me?" I ask.

"No."

My head stops spinning, and my heavy breathing evens out. Oddly enough, I believe the Selell. "Then what do you want from me?" I squeeze the doorknob. "Why have you taken me prisoner?"

"You're not my prisoner," he says with composed calm.

"Then why have you locked me inside this manor?" My eyes travel across the high ceiling. The sight causes the cold and emptiness to seize me. A shiver streaks down my spine.

But once again, the Selell's lips are sealed. I notice that he is not only frugal with words, but he is a subtle being. His eyes shift subtly to the right of me. Subtly the lines in his neck tighten. He shifts swiftly, and he's so close to me that I feel the heat emanating from his skin. I find this odd because, from what I've been taught, the body of a Selell is ice cold.

"Give me your light, Adore. If that will make you trust me."

I'm caught off guard by his seductive tone. I blink myself out of a stunned pause. "You never told me how you knew my name," I whisper, but my words still manage to echo in the hollowness. I'm determined to remain vigilant because I still sense deception from him.

He glowers at me. "I can't say."

I gulp. "But why?"

"Because I don't want you to be afraid of me."

"I'm already afraid of you," I confess.

"But I don't want you to be."

"Then let me leave."

Once again, he exhibits all the nuances I once noticed. He balls up his fists. I notice how his fingers slip against the inside of his hand. His palms are sweating.

"If I could, I would," he says after a long moment of observing my curious expression.

I look from his hands to his face. The two creases between his eyes have sunk deeper.

"Why are you so conflicted?" I ask.

"I don't know." He looks away from me and steps backward. Is it anger that now colors his expression? "But we're both stuck here, so get used to it." Then he's gone.

I feel deserted by the Selell with the white hair, by my father, my mother, and my sisters. Every part of me turns heavy—my heart, my head, all of my limbs. Regardless, I carry myself as fast as I can back up the stairs, through the long hallway, and back to the room from which I came.

But as soon as I step over the threshold, I come to an abrupt stop. A different covering is stretched over the bed. It's thick, white, and fluffy, and the hem sweeps the floor. A glass-topped wooden table is positioned against the wall beneath a hanging mirror near the doorway where I'm standing, and two tall candles burn on top of it, one at each corner. The candlelight casts its orange brilliance against the white wall. I am almost convinced that my captor has made an effort to make me comfortable, but I don't want to be contented; I want to go home.

I run to the bed and fall into the depths of its cushiony softness. I flip on my back, close my eyes, and try to contact Cl'auta. Once again, I do not succeed. I try to reach Falu and Pan'a'tua, but they do not respond either.

"Na'ta," I whisper. Na'ta—who is called Navi on Earth—is my last hope. I flip around to bury my face in the plush pillow. I'm holding my breath when, in the most splendid moment thus far, I hear Na'ta.

Although she sounds far off, she whimpers, "Ad'ru, help me."

I fly off the bed and stand firmly. "I'k suk'ne'-tu!" I shout, frantically twisting my neck to search in every direction. "I'm here!"

I wait. Na'ta has the speed. She will come and sweep me out of here; the stranger with the white hair and dark eyes will not notice that I'm gone. The thought of leaving him makes my heart float up to my throat. I smash my eyes closed. I'm confused. I *want* to be saved by Navi, don't I?

The longer I stand here, the more it becomes clear that Na'ta is not coming for me. I flop back onto the bed and once again bury my face into the pillow.

Time passes. My head is filled with memories of home until I'm running at full stride across the green blades of grass that layer my beloved Enu. This is the high grass that leads to the Meadow of Showers. My giggles pinch the air around me. Never-ceasing droplets of warm rain pelt my skin. I'm laughing because Tryst is chasing me. I'm in the part of the field where the grass grows high enough to swipe the bottom of my chin. It tickles, which is another reason I'm laughing so hard that my stomach tightens.

"Got you!" Tryst shouts as his large orange hands wrangle me into him from behind.

I'm caught. The chase is over. We both let go of our legs and fall onto the grass.

"You are fast, Ad'ru," he says in English.

He obeys Ce'lah'ime. She tells him to speak to me only in the humans' language to remind both of us that I am not fully of this world.

Only I *am* fully of this world! I am here, perfectly contained in happiness. Tryst flips on his side. His orange eyes meet my emerald eyes. I'm still smiling. Yes, I love Tryst. We can endlessly explore our orb, running, jumping, swimming, diving, sliding, and lying side by side just like this.

One of his hands rests on my belly. His fingers draw tiny circles on my belly through my wet white pal'k. But there's something different about the way he's touching me. My eyes are closed, and I compulsively suck in air between my teeth. His touch is so sensual, and my thighs long for him. I have felt this sensation before. It's what Cl'auta felt when the Selell Ze Feldis mounted her on the Ridge of Way.

I force my eyes open to see what's happening to me, because I don't understand why Tryst is lighting this fire within me. However, it's a pure white face that's looking down upon me. I'm shivering because, oddly, the air turns cold and because of the anticipation that inflicts me. His fingers remain on my belly, but each one slowly creeps toward my face. I curl my neck forward to see what he's doing to me. I don't understand why he makes me feel this way.

"Stop," I feebly plead.

In truth, I don't want him to stop. I'm eager to learn what his hand will do next as it snakes up between the bone that separates my breasts. The white-haired Selell's hand freezes, but he lowers his face closer to mine. This Selell's breath is extremely cold.

"Are you dead?" I whisper.

Although he's close and my words reach his ears, he doesn't honor me with an answer. Instead, he snakes his fingers up the round of one of my breasts. My eyes expand. I gulp. What is he doing to me? Why? His lips part at seeing what I see. My brown skin shows through the wet garment. His fingers circle my nipple, which has never been touched before, and I tickle all over. It's not the sort of delight that makes me want to laugh.

"You know what we are, don't you?" he asks.

I can't answer him. I can't take my eyes off his fingers and what they're doing to me. "Please, stop."

"You want me near you, don't you?" he whispers.

"No… I mean yes." I shake my head, confused.

His lips are so close that they narrowly touch mine. I swallow hard in anticipation of what is to come.

"You want me near you, don't you?" he repeats.

I'm unable to speak.

Then the white-haired Selell's lips move. "Ad'ru," he says, but it's not his voice that I hear.

"Na'ta?" I gasp.

Instantly, the white-haired Selell disappears. I'm no longer in the Meadow of Whispers. I'm standing on dry, cracked ground. A blood-red sun bears down over me in this desolate forest. It's brazenly hot, so hot that my throat heats up with every intake of the sooty air.

"Help me, Ad'ru," Na'ta whimpers from behind me.

I whip around. My eyes travel up toward the branches of the tree, dreading what I can't avoid seeing. The branches spiral, twist, and turn in precarious ways. The smoky gray wood looks smooth but is sharp at its edges.

You have to come and free me… Na'ta moans.

Tueka'lek'mak! I cry.

She's staked through the heart by a branch high on one of the trees. More branches coil tightly around her arms, legs, and even her torso, holding her captive. I clutch my chest at the sight of her face. Her normal pink lips are blue, and they shiver as if she is ice cold in the stifling heat. I can tell that she is weak and barely clinging to the little strength she has left.

I try to push off on my toes to lift off and save her, but instead of flying, my eyes flick open. I'm still on the bed in the room where I am being held captive. The Selell with white hair is standing over me with his usual facial expression. The corners of his mouth are pulled down, and his brows are furrowed. Although I'm shaken by leaving Na'ta, I'm also paralyzed by that look on the Selell's face.

"Bad dream?" he asks.

I wait for him to lean back, but he doesn't budge. "No," I answer him in a small voice. "I don't dream. What I experienced was real."

"All of it?" He lifts his eyebrows curiously. He knows what happened in the Meadow of Showers.

I skip a breath, remembering the way he touched me.

"You're not used to sleeping?" he says.

It's strange that he asks that. I want to answer

him, but my instincts tell me to be very cautious. How could he invade my mind and be with me in Enu?

He takes a step back so that I can sit up. I cannot erase the sight of Na'ta in the tree from my memory. How did that happen to her? When last we faced each other, she visited me in the East Orb, at Father's cavern; we stood on the plank, gazing out over the White Sea, and I told her all about Cl'auta and Falu. This was after Falu had been fed the mirk by the Selell, who deceived her.

"You must release me," I say as I move with great speed to stand. I get close to him and clamp my hand around his wrist. I hurry to give him the light, rendering him incapable of wriggling out of my grasp.

He goes stiff as he studies the hold I have on him. I'm also caught off guard by what's happening inside me. I was growing accustomed to being continuously cold, but the shift in my body temperature since I grabbed his wrist is alarming. I'm warm, and it's not just any warmth; the sunrays that fall over Enu have exploded inside me, filling me from the tip of my toes to the crown of my head. It's the best feeling ever, better than basking in the Enuian sun itself.

"Who are you?" I ask past my tightened throat.

"You know who I am, Adore," he says with incredible repose.

"But you haven't revealed your name."

"I can't."

"Why not?"

"You'll hate me."

I determinedly shake my head. "I haven't the capacity to hate."

He nods. "I know."

"You do?"

"I know a lot about you, Ad'ru, and you know a lot about me."

Now I'm very confused. "I don't understand." I hope he'll elaborate.

He lifts his arm, the one I'm holding. "There are seven daughters of the house of Benel, and you have the power to affect." His eyes examine each of my fingers. "We have that in common. I've made men who've called for my head be loyal beyond degree, and women who've regarded me with spite, love me."

I am greatly disturbed by this revelation. "Then you've used the power of light to do evil." I release his wrist, but he quickly grabs mine.

He squeezes my arm tightly but not so much that it hurts. "Why does that make me evil?"

He pulls me into him. I'm light on my feet, and my body easily cooperates with his demand.

"You're forcing your will upon an unsuspecting creature," I answer. My head is no longer dizzy from the force of our touching, and the warmth of his touch might as well be a million miles away. "You are right. If you are evil, then I will not hate you, but I cannot love you."

His hand tightens around my wrist. "I didn't ask for your love," he hisses like an Earth serpent.

"Then what do you want from me?" I've never been this angry.

A tiny smile forms on his lips, and once again, I sense deception from him. "I need you not to hate me."

"Release me. Then I'll be sure not to."

He snorts. "You still refuse to acknowledge what we are, don't you?"

"What are we?" I ask.

He answers by smashing his lips onto mine. The lightheadedness is back. Our mouths are warm. His tongue is hot upon mine. This, what we're doing, seems natural. I've kissed Tryst thousands of times, but not once has it ever felt like this.

He pulls away and puts his lips to my ear. "You're not making this easy. Adore, we are bonded."

"What?" I gasp.

He is a peculiar being with silky white hair and skin, and lips that are delicately pink. I never would have guessed the creature I would be bonded to would have such an appearance. I've always been partial to skin that glows like the sapphire stone during the season of the Tilt. Like Ast'e'ku, a mank'tak—or Enuian male—who shimmers like the Velvet Stream in the South Orb. Ast'e'ku's nose curves like the beak of the bird called "the parrot," and he uses his beautiful nostrils to blow blessings of bliss upon all who request it. He's a beautiful Enuian, unique and desirable to the eyes, and he is considered perfection to the heart because he bears happiness. Although I cannot say that I'm not drawn to this Selell, his beauty is novel, very near to that of Pan'a'tua.

"But I cannot bond with you," I confess. "I have to leave. My sister needs me."

His lips are still against my ear, and he doesn't loosen his hold on me. "Do you know what I do, Adore? I take what I want."

"And what do you give?" I automatically ask. I

don't recognize the sound of my own voice. It's small and desperate.

"Ha! Nothing," he bellows.

"And that satisfies you?"

"I want you here with me. If I let you leave, then I won't have what I want." His eyes narrow to slits. He's threatening me with that look.

My defiance is reflexive. I call the power of light to my fingertips. "If you keep me here against my will, you won't have me. I will battle you, Selell, and I will not lose."

His lips stretch into a weak but telling smile. "Well then…"

The door and the stained-glass window fly open. A black sky, which lacks moons and stars, settles over the earth. If it weren't for the long poles topped by bulbous light fixtures casting their beams in the darkness, the red-brick cobblestone walkway would be pitch black. The lawn holds limestone statues carved into human forms posed in precarious positions. These sculptures intermingle with headstones with names and dates etched into the rock.

The Selell steps back to give me passage. "You're free to go. But I have to warn you—the humans have gone mad. It's not safe to be out there all by your lonesome."

"The humans have gone mad?" I ask, quite perplexed by his assertion.

"The sun has pulled a Houdini."

My frown turns more austere. I do believe he's using local vernacular.

"It disappeared," he says after interpreting my expression.

"But why?" I whisper as I observe how dark it is beyond the confines of this large, beautiful estate. "The sun has been promised to the earth. It will never leave."

"All promises are made to be broken." His shrug is indifferent.

I shake my head. "No, not this one."

Regardless, because of the darkness, I am hesitant to make my escape. The cold of the night settles upon me. At this very moment, an emotion takes root inside me. The farther I try to see into the darkness that falls over the earth, the more identifiable the emotion becomes.

"But you'll come with me?" I ask nervously.

He's grinning again, and I take that as a good sign. "I'll go with you as long as you promise me one thing."

I feel my eyebrows pull into a guarded frown. "What is that?"

"Promise not to ask my name. I'll tell you when I'm ready."

It's a simple enough request. I am aware that he is someone who practices evil, but I cannot dismiss the power of the bond. Other than my sisters, I feel that this Selell will be my safest companion.

"And you'll help me find my sisters?" I clarify.

"Yes." His answer is resolute.

"Then I promise not to ask you your name."

CHAPTER 3

THE DECISION
ADORE

T he white-haired Selell offers me shoes before we depart to find Na'ta. They are sandals, but they conceal my toes with a tiny strap around the ankles. They are green, and the first pair of shoes I have ever worn.

The Selell walks beside me, holding my hand to keep me warm. What an honorable gesture. The radiant Selell is a silent being in words only, not in thoughts. He often gazes upon me with a confused expression. I do not wish to know his thoughts. They are reserved for those with the power of the mind. His silence is welcome, especially as I absorb all that surrounds us. I cannot believe it; the time has come for me, Ad'ru, the first daughter of Felix Benel and Ce'lah'ime, to walk upon the earth.

My swiftness is limited in this universe, and I find it frustrating. Together we move past wild trees that resemble black giants lurking in the lightless forest. I can barely see what's before me. I'm relying solely on the Selell's guidance. A caustic odor lingers in the air.

"What is that smell?" I ask my companion.

"It's a lot of things." His fingers tighten around my hand.

"What are those things you're referring to?" Even in the dark, I see his white face glance down at me. He's a very tall creature. He lords over me, and I feel trapped in his gaze.

"Shit and death," he says.

I can see a bit of his teeth in the dark. I assume he's lifted his top lip into that sinister smile of his. "Death?" I'm intrigued. I've never seen death. "Dead humans?"

He snorts, amused. "And animals…"

"You sound pleased by that."

"I do?" he says in an extremely inquisitive tone.

I sense he is teasing me. He comes to a sudden stop and turns to face me. His nose, lips, and eyes are very close to mine.

"You really are innocent, aren't you?" he asks and slides the tip of his warm finger across my top lip. "But you don't look innocent." He leans closer. His nose grazes my lips. "Or smell innocent."

I allow myself to relish what's happening to me. My throat is tight, my head is light, and I'm fighting the desire to touch and taste tongues with him once again.

"Destiny has played the cruelest joke on you, Ad'ru. Clarity has Ze Feldis. Fawn has Artiste. Glo has Finn. You've got me." He snorts cynically.

Do it... My heart begs, needing him to put his mouth on mine. Yet my head attempts to eradicate that desire. "You are very well acquainted with my sisters and me, are you not?" I can barely speak through my heavy breathing.

"I'm not as acquainted with you as I thought."

"As you *thought*? How could you be acquainted with me at all? You've never known me."

His teeth flash in the dark. The look is so tricky, it makes a shiver run up and down my spine.

"Are you a sinister being?" I'm forced to ask, dreading the answer.

"That requires a subjective answer," he slyly replies.

"Are you always so vague, Selell?" I'm frustrated, so my voice is harsh.

This time he lets out a shrieking laugh that

bounces off the dusky trees. He's amused by my frustration. But he has a peculiar sort of amusement. I can't help but press my hand over the place where his body once carried a vital human heart. The i'lek'u pours out of my palm and flows into him, absorbing all the thoughts and feelings that make this Selell a living being. Because of the light, I can fully see his face. He's terrified.

"No, don't," he feebly protests.

He tries to pull away from my touch, but it's too late. I've latched on, and there's no breaking the link.

He is confounded at the moment, struggling to regain full consciousness. But the light reveals that he wants something from me, and I cannot determine what that is. However, he can't hide what is strong in him. He's greatly afflicted by arrogance, pride, and a deep desire to obtain all that he lusts for, and that includes *me*. I quickly remove my hand. The Selell collapses onto the damp soil, clutching his black shirt at the spot where my palm rested. I kneel beside him without allowing my knees to make contact with the corroded earth.

"What the hell was that?" he roars in anger.

"You've been deceitful," I apologetically say. "I needed truth to journey farther with you."

He struggles to stand while brushing the mud off the back of his trousers. "I can't believe I don't want to kill you."

I'm very shocked to hear that, mainly because he says it so casually.

"But do you know what I want to do to you instead?" He grabs my waist and pulls me into him.

My nose is pushed up against his collarbone. I smell his shirt; the scent is fresh and sweet. He presses my hips closer to his, and I can feel a solid mass against me.

He snorts. "You have no idea, do you?"

The dark, the Selell, and the impure stench mixed with his sweet odor makes me want to connect with this creature in such an inordinate way. Is this lust that infects me? In this moment, I don't even recognize myself as Ad'ru, the keeper of the light. So I force my head to stop spinning and my heart to stop fluttering. I am full of good. He's touched by evil.

His wicked sneer returns but not for long. He whips his face around to look to the right of me. He's alarmed, and I wonder why.

"Kill the light," he barely whispers.

I direct the i'lek'u back deep inside me.

Without asking permission, the Selell lifts me

and cradles me in his arms. "Let's get the hell out of here," he says before streaking off.

The persistent darkness annoys me. The sun hasn't made an appearance since it descended when I first arrived on Earth. But the scent of the wild trees and rank soil passes, and within a very short period of time, he's standing on a sidewalk that runs along a street. Here, among the rows of stone buildings with bulging balconies and more street-lamps, the Selell reluctantly sets me back on my feet. We take a while to pull apart, but I notice that his heart is beating, and fast. On Earth, a Selell is dead, a being with no heartbeat or moving blood. Other than his brain, his organs have shut down. So his heartbeat is odd, but I feel this is not the time to question him, especially since he takes my hand again, and its warmth soothes away the cold.

"This way," he says before stepping off the side-walk, landing one foot on the cobblestone street.

"Wait!" I shout, now clinging tightly to his arm. He looks at me, puzzled, and I wonder why. "My father warned me to be careful when crossing modern roads on Earth. Vehicles can be a danger to me."

At first, the Selell appears more puzzled. In his moment of pause, I finally notice the people—there are lots of them. Then he throws his head back and laughs so loudly that the passing humans eye him with a certain amount of disdain, which I find alarming. This time, nothing sinister colors the tone of his laugh.

"Did your father also tell you to look both ways before crossing the street?" He's still grinning, amused.

"Yes, he did," I reply, remembering that. "Although he didn't say that precisely. But his words were very similar."

He's still grinning at me in that peculiar way.

"What is it?" I ask, but he's distracted by a number of humans passing us in a single-file line.

"It's too late to repent," their voices rise in unison. "The sun is blood, judgment is soon, and then the pit."

Their brown and yellow faces are slathered with black ashes. The energy they emit is strong with fear and despair. Little ones trail behind them, and they are also terrified.

My companion snorts then twists his neck to bark over his shoulder at them, "The sun isn't blood, you idiots!"

"You shouldn't say that to them," I scold, keeping my voice low.

"I thought you were a proponent of the truth."

"Proponent of the truth?" I give some thought to the vernacular he's used. "Do you mean that I'm an advocate for truth?"

After taking a moment to study me with those amused eyes of his, he grunts, "Ha," and then tugs me toward the street. "We should get moving. I won't let you get hit by a car, Adore."

We're almost across the street before I'm able to part my lips to object. However, I decide against saying anything since we've made it across safely.

"See?" He turns as we step onto the sidewalk. "I told you I'll keep you safe, although I can't take credit for it."

He points, and I look where his long white finger directs my eyes. Something that looks like a long wooden bench is in the middle of the road.

"Traffic is blocked," he says.

A number of humans zip past us. Although their eyes search in all directions, they all study me for a number of seconds before shifting to my companion. I am curious as to what is so puzzling about us. Can they tell that we are not fully of their species? The humans continue to regard us curiously, but I cannot focus on them because I can't take my eyes off the white-haired Selell. He is apprehensive and peering ahead very judiciously. We've increased our pace, and he takes a long look over his shoulder. Before I can see what he is looking at, he tugs me into him and curls an arm around me, pulling me closer.

"This way," he whispers. He makes haste to guide me past a glass door into one of the establishments lining the long, busy sidewalk.

We're safely inside an establishment. The electrical lighting is dim. A number of humans sit at square, white- and gold-swirled marble-topped tables. Each of them has a quietness about them— no, a *solemnity*. Like the people outside, they're observing us. I watch two male-type human beings whisper to each other without taking their eyes off me. Then their eyes regard the white-haired Selell. We are receiving too much attention from beings who are capable of inflicting so much pain on those who are different from them. That cannot be good for us.

"What sort of place is this?" I ask. The ambiance makes me nervous.

I lift my palm, intending to abolish any negative energy and replace it with peace and benevolence. But before I can release the i'lek'u, my companion obstructs my hand. His long fingers completely cover mine.

"What in the hell do you think you're doing?" he gripes.

The two men are still watching us.

"Why are they looking at us in that manner? I detect evil intentions."

Once again, he tosses his head back to laugh. I notice how his lengthy tresses spread across his broad shoulders. Some of the mank'taks wear their hair in such a way, but his locks are more graceful, cascading from his scalp like the crystal clear liquid of the Geng'ket Falls. He turns quiet and gently swipes the backs of his long fingers across my cheek. I'm mesmerized by how his now-dark-green eyes have grown lighter since I last looked into them.

"They're watching you because, even before life, humans regard beauty; even when shit's like this."

"I'm sorry, I don't understand how you are using the word 'shit.'"

"You never heard the word 'shit' before?"

"I have, but not in the context that you just used it in."

He lowers his face to meet mine. "This is the shit they're in. The sun is missing, and they're slowly going insane." His eyes roam the room. "I give them a solid month before they snap and start killing each other. It's their nature."

I shake my head, refusing to believe the apparent truth. "No. The Creator gave the earth a sun. It can't just disappear."

"Hey, take it up with your *creator*, not me. Hell." He lifts his arms and shakes his hands. "I thrive in the night."

I scowl at him. "Apparently this is all amusing to you."

"Not really." He gazes at me. "But you, Ad'ru. You amuse me."

There... I watch his eyes grow perceptibly lighter until he twists around to search behind him. He focuses on the glass door then turns his alarmed expression to me.

"What?" I ask. He's transferred his panic.

"Here." Without permission, he gathers my hair and twists the long, wavy strands, working very fast. When he's done, my long locks are knotted at the nape of my neck.

I reach back to touch the tight ball, wondering why he did that and how. He curls his arm around mine and guides me to a stool at a very high counter. We both sit with our backs to the door, and the Selell once again lowers his face to mine.

"You want to find your sister Na'ta?" he asks in a low whisper.

His nearness has taken my breath away. I'm only capable of nodding.

"Remember that," he says as I hear the whistle of air when the door opens.

A harsh voice shouts, "Exgesis!"

The Selell is no longer seated beside me. My eyes shift to the human behind the counter. He's frozen in place, staring straight ahead. A loud crash rings out. I whip around to see the white-haired Selell has collided into one of the marble-topped tables, breaking it in large chunks. That name, Exgesis, repeats in my head, and I squeeze my eyes shut tightly. I've heard it before, but where?

"This is going to be too easy," says another Selell with black shaggy hair. He is glowering down at the white-haired Selell.

The impact has left the white-haired Selell groggy. The black-haired Selell's hand shifts to the inside of his long black coat. When it's visible again, it's clutching a silver-bladed dagger. A few humans in the room watch in shock; others scramble to get out of the way. This new Selell has tainted the air with violence, and he means to put an end to his target.

"You don't want to do this, Chex," my Selell says as he struggles to stand. "Name your price."

"Zero," the aggressor replies without deliberation. "And yes." He nods and lifts his eyebrows at him. "I want to do this,"

My Selell streaks out of the aggressor's trap, leaving a white shadow in his trail. These phantoms chase each other around the room, leaving destruction in their path. Chairs and parts of tables whip through the air, slamming into walls and shattering. My eyes work to keep up until I'm facing the dagger-gripping, black-haired Selell. I gasp as a hard body presses against my back, and the soft hair of my Selell swipes my cheek.

"When are you going to stop hiding behind girls and kids, you coward?" the black-haired Selell scoffs.

Exegesis… I ponder.

The Selell called Chex glares at me with his pitch-black eyes, sending a shiver down my spine. His nostrils flare as he leans in, taking a long, deliberate inhale, his brows knitting together in confusion or recognition. I can practically feel the stench of death and the blood of others clinging to him like a second skin.

"You're one of those sisters?" he growls, his

voice thick with menace. It feels more like a command than a question, but I'm frozen in place, too terrified to respond.

Chex shifts his focus, turning those dark, dangerous eyes onto the Selell standing beside me. "How did you acquire this one, Exgesis?" he demands.

The name slips from my lips like a whisper, "Exgesis…" It hits me like a wave, crashing over the confusion in my mind. The truth starts to unfurl, slowly, chillingly. My Selell isn't just any vampire; he's *the* Exgesis. The revelation sinks in, tightening the grip of fear around my throat.

"Ha!" the black-haired Selell snorts. He points the sharp tip of his weapon at Exgesis. "You don't know who this bastard is?"

That object is so very dangerous in his hand, and I've gathered my bearings enough to touch his wrist. "Could you please put that away?" I ask, trying to steady my voice as I flood him with as much light as possible.

"No," he says. "I know you're working your magic on me, and don't worry your pretty little head. It's having an effect, but you'll never get me to let down my guard around that bastard. *You* shouldn't either."

"Come on, Chex; this is not the place for your grudge." Exgesis scans the room.

All the humans watch us, stunned. Many of them are clutching tiny square gadgets.

The black-haired Selell named Chex laughs loudly and then takes an exaggerated breath. "You care about humans now, do you?"

"This isn't about you, Chex!" Exgesis barks.

"Put your hands up!" the human behind the counter demands.

All three of us look at him. He's pointing a handgun at Chex's head. Without warning, Chex moves. When the streak stops, he's holding the handgun and aiming it at the human while keeping the sharp point of the dagger aimed at Exgesis. Loud gasps and a chorus of whispers erupt. The humans are baffled by what they've witnessed. This entire scene doesn't sit well with me either.

"Chex," I say, holding up my palms.

"Yes?" He's overstating his agreeableness.

I'm immobilized, trapped by his menacing, intriguing eyes. "They're afraid—the humans are. We should leave. Leave our matters to those who are aware of them?"

He grins, showing a straight line of white teeth. "Humph. I thought I liked the one who set my ass on fire, but the diplomatic approach is…" He sucks air through his teeth.

As I flinch, Exgesis draws me into him. Chex's eyes don't miss this, and his grin grows broader, showing his amusement in the same sinister way Exgesis often does. The two of them carry similar traces of darkness.

"Certainly," he sings facetiously as he whips his shoulders forward and slides the dagger back inside his long black coat. He fixes his slanting eyes on me. "You just come on over here with me, and we'll be on our way."

Now it's Exgesis who's laughing. He sounds so wicked that I twist around to see if he's vexed with ek'et'ru. I sigh with relief because I cannot see the red haze of death swirling in his eyes.

The two Selells are not concerned by the number of people who have gathered on the side-walk behind the cracked window. Instead, the Selells' eyes anxiously search the street.

"I'm taking you back to Ze Feldis and Elo. Let's go," Chex says, curving his head toward the door.

Hearing the name Ze Feldis sounds like salvation. He can lead me to Cl'auta.

"Enough!" Exgesis roars so loudly that it feels as if the earth shakes.

The fear trapped in the room has become so strong that it grips me. I can no longer bear it, and I reach inside myself to gather the light of peace. Chex watches me pucker my lips, and before he can figure out what I'm doing, I blow as hard as I can. Blinding light explodes, filling the room. When the i'lek'u subsides, a soft yellow shimmer settles over the space. Every human is subdued. And this time, my power works fully on both Selells. Exgesis's hold on me is no longer tight and possessive; instead, his grasp is full and desperate.

Chex is compelled to take staggering steps over to the counter to drop the handgun. "What the hell did you just do to me?" His body is weak because he's fighting the good that now constrains the evil inside him. To remain standing, he rests on the wood railing.

"What you're feeling will pass if you stop struggling against the light," I say.

He grimaces. "You don't know what you're doing."

I'm taken by surprise by something rushing toward me, and I'm lifted off the floor. There's a sharp change in the temperature. The warmth that Exgesis's touch stirs within me is gone. I am no longer engulfed by the i'lek'u. There are no broken tables or chairs, and the fearful humans are far away from here. I look up and see the murky night sky.

"Better," Chex says, stretching his lengthy neck from one side to the other. "Now, that sure does change the nature of our future association," he says sarcastically. "So are you coming or not?"

"Wait," I nearly shout, hampered by frustration. I'm confused and missing the warmth of my Selell. Where is this place that the Selell Chex has taken me?

We're on a grimy concrete bridge stretched over stale gray liquid. I'm appalled by what I see. I have never seen water that dirty. The humans have clearly neglected the source from which it flows. Then a horn wails. The sound makes both me and the bridge tremble.

Once it's quiet again and my trembling has turned to shivering, I ask, "But you can take me to Ze Feldis?"

"And I can take you to Na'ta," Exgesis whispers.

He's here. The bitter cold has yet again passed away. He's against my backside, and I want to fall into him, swim in the warmth. Chex curls his top lip. For a moment, I think he's going to attack Exgesis, the bringer of the warmth, but Chex stays where he stands.

"What was her name?" Chex pinches his chin as if he's calling up his memory. "Fawn. That's it, isn't it?" He sets his gaze on me. "That's your sister?"

"Yes," I squeak in a high-pitched voice. Just hearing her name makes me feel closer to her. "You know Falu?"

He points toward us with his chin. "He does too. Before you decide to go off and bed this fellow, you should know all about how *familiar* he is with Fawn, or Falu, or whatever the hell her name is."

My Selell turns me around to face him. The movement is so fast I can hardly feel it happening. These creatures are quicker than we are on Earth.

"I knew your sister Falu. We were… acquaint-ed," Exgesis says very calmly. The look in his eyes pleads for me to hear his words over Chex's.

I look into his eyes. My thoughts are thrown off track because I see that they're green again. It's also become apparent who this Selell is. "You're Lario Exgesis…?" I find myself gasping for every breath I take.

All of a sudden, I feel trapped between two dangerous creatures. But with what I remember about the one I'm facing, he is the most treacherous. He fed Falu the mirk, human blood. He deceived her into loving him, and now he is the one dark fleck in Cl'auta's heart because, more than life itself, she wants him dead.

"Bingo," Chex coolly says. He's moved closer; I feel his presence hovering behind me.

"We've come this far, and I haven't done anything to hurt you, have I?" Exgesis whispers in desperation.

"Just because he hasn't doesn't mean he won't," Chex adds.

My poor face, which has come to display expressions I have no control over, frowns hard. "I'm not sure. You have been hurting me by keeping me away from my sisters."

"I'm helping you find your sister!" he shouts. His eyes are ablaze. He releases a hard breath and calmly asks, "You want to get to Na'ta, don't you?"

I swallow hard as I'm only barely able to nod.

"I'm the only one who can take you there."

"And why is that, Exgesis?" Chex touches my shoulder, and his hand is cold. "Listen, love. I'm giving you an easy out. Take it. Usually he'll let you go over *your* dead body. Never *his*. And by God—

little 'G' then 'od'—if Exgesis is ever willing to let you walk, then pigs are flying."

Even though I can't see him, I know Chex is flashing that wicked grin of his. That look is natural for him.

But the question that Chex asked is very valid.

"Yes, why are you the only one who can take me to Na'ta? Surely Cl'auta can?" I ask Exgesis.

"Because the portal opens in…"—Exgesis takes one hand off of me to twist his arm and study the face of the timepiece that's strapped around his wrist—"seven minutes, exactly."

"Where there's a will, there's a way!" shouts Chex.

I'm swept off of my feet, carried so quickly that my head grows weak. When I come to a stop, Chex is squeezing me close with his forearm lodged against my belly. But he only has me for a matter of seconds. I'm pulled out of his grasp by a stealthy force that sends me flying across the concrete bridge, but I gain control of myself before I slam into the metal guards. I gaze up the path and see Chex straddling Lario Exgesis. They're struggling over an object. I gasp as soon as I make out what it is: the dagger. Chex has the tip of it aimed at Exgesis's heart, and Exgesis has Chex by the wrist, struggling to keep from being gutted. Even from where I stand, this contest looks easy for Chex.

"No!" I aim my palm at the Selells, striking them both with a more powerful dose of the light.

At first they freeze, and then, to my relief, Chex drops the dagger. The metal clinks on the icy asphalt. The light has made them groggy, so they struggle to rise to their feet. I race over and lay my hands on Exgesis's chest. He may be untrustworthy and he may be the reason why Na'ta is being held captive, but he is my warmth and my bond, and, according to my vision, my sister needs me.

"I'll go with you," I tell Exgesis.

With my declaration, Chex streaks away to escape the light.

My lifeblood is rushing through me. I've never been so uncertain about anything. I cannot discount what this Selell is capable of, but my father once told me to choose instinct over fear. And in this instance, I'm following the warmth, which, to my relief, is flooding me once again.

CHAPTER 4

THE DOWNPOUR
ADORE

"Will you let me carry you?" the Selell, Lario Exgesis, asks timidly.

He seems more careful now that I know his true identity. His crimes against my sisters and their bonds are great and certainly heinous. Fate was not kind to bond us, but bonded we are.

I nod stiffly because he stopped holding my hand to ask me that question. The tiny amount of cold afflicting my skin is akin to torture. This temperature is new to me, and I simply cannot tolerate it. He must know that, because as soon as I give my consent, he sweeps me up in his arms, and we're on our way.

I close my eyes and allow his warmth to help me

pretend that I am home. I visualize myself racing through the Forest of Whispers where the purple versa trees grow. The sunlight filters through their rounded leaves and kisses every part of my face. But I've never been in the Forest of Whispers with this tingling in my stomach and fire in my thighs. Not with my instincts overruling my reason.

"Ad'ru?" the Selell whispers in my fantasy.

"Yes" glides past my parted lips.

"Open your eyes."

I peel them open only to find him grimacing into my face. So quickly, I'm becoming familiar with the lines, curves, and expressions of his face.

"We're here," he mutters.

I look away from him and all around me. We're back where we were, across the street from the establishment where the two Selells battled. Two white cars with spiraling red and blue lights on top and the word 'Police' painted in blue along the side are parked in front. The i'lek'u still flourishes behind the glass window where four men in blue shirts huddle around the man who drew the handgun and pointed it at Chex. I'm positive the humans cannot see the i'lek'u even though they are affected by it.

I search for some sort of portal, but all I see are

more buildings with pergolas, tall windows, and balconies with decorative iron or wooden rails. It would be easy to see the portal glow because most of the establishments that line the street are not lit from the inside or outside. "I don't see the portal." I squint out of frustration more than vision impairment.

"Give it time," he quietly says, glaring straight through the window at the men in blue shirts.

My thoughts are still overactive. I wonder if I made the right decision. At this very moment, I could be with Cl'auta. I understood when Chex said, "Where there's a will, there's a way." Cl'auta would have figured out a way to get to Na'ta. Surely her powers combined with my other sisters' could aid me in finding Na'ta and bringing her safely home.

Home? The notion of home has become obscure ever since I laid eyes on this Selell whose crimes continue to list themselves in my head. He's the being who tried to dissolve the love between Cl'auta and Ze Feldis with lies, and he used deceit in his attempts to steal *The Book of the Seven Seeds*. Yet here I stand, beside him. I trust this Selell, but I find him far from trustworthy. I'm unwisely willing to risk danger to remain in his company. This could be a weakness of my humanity, but the impulse is too strong to resist.

"You tried to kill my sister," I mutter in the silence that lingers between us.

"Are you referring to Fawn?" he asks, still looking straight ahead.

I blink, taken aback by his response. "Have you tried to kill any of my other sisters?"

"I haven't tried to kill any of them, not even Fawn." He looks at me. "And that is the truth."

"Then why did you feed her the mirk?"

His scowl intensifies. "I count it as one of my transgressions. One day I'll pay for them all, but will you make that time now?"

"Why did you deceive her?" My tongue swells from anticipation.

He runs a hand through his hair as he considers my question. Then he looks away from me to stare straight ahead. "There," he says with a sigh of relief.

I trace his line of sight, and I'm surprised to see that the portal is the cracked window. "How did you know about this portal?" I watch him with scrutiny.

"I don't have time to answer your questions. Do you want to save your sister or not?"

My feet are like two boulders. This Selell is devious. If I elect to move forward with him, then I'll be choosing danger. But Na'ta's distress seizes me from beyond the doorway. It intensifies the longer I stand here contemplating whether I'm brave enough to leap into danger.

"I will follow you." I sigh, surrendering.

The Selell, Exgesis, tugs me across the narrow street without looking both ways. We bolt toward the doorway that sets the entire window aglow. The human who was behind the counter stabs a finger in our direction, and the men in blue look our way, but we leap through the portal before any of them can move toward us.

My face splits the warm, fluid rays that carry us from one dimension to the next. I see the white-haired Selell in front of me. He knows exactly where he's going; he's leading me down a specific path. This journey is not a short one. The farther we go, the more apprehensive I grow about putting my destiny in his hands, but there's no turning back.

Finally the light disappears, and the Selell and I are standing in an open field. The ground feels strange beneath the soles of my shoes, so I look down. Oh, how I regret looking! It's wet and mushy, black- and gray-flecked dirt layered thinly by slimy green moss. It's disgusting and foul and neglected by those who were given this universe.

But there's daylight here, so I gaze up to see the sun hidden behind a dense veil of bulging, pallid clouds that dart rapidly across the sky. The speed with which they move is so spectacular that I can't peel my eyes away. I have never seen such a thing.

"What universe is this?" I observe it in a heightened state of awe. I turn to look at Exgesis when he takes too long to reply.

"This is Rnv," he mutters. He clears his throat. "Of the Mtknv."

"Mtknv. I've never heard of this species. Are they hostile?" I ask.

He glares at me with the same hostile expression. "Yes."

That look on his face makes me shudder. I gulp. "And are we here because this species is holding my sister captive?"

"Yes," he snaps, short on patience. He is definitely irritated by my questions.

"But why?" I press, refusing to let him intimidate me.

"How would I know that?"

I pin my eyes on him as silence falls between us. I fight the urge to argue with him. His demeanor incites such a drive within me. I feel drops of water pelt my skin, and I look up. I glance at Exgesis, and he's looking upward too.

"We should take cover," he mutters.

I agree. There's energy up there somewhere, and it knows we're here. We trot into the forest at a regular human's speed. We are shaded by lofty, grim trees with branches that flop lazily like the earth's weeping willows. The sheer number of them makes for a ghostly sight. The green is a continuous web, connecting one tree to the next and forming a vast dark plane that threatens to swallow us whole.

Yes, the forest is dark, and the deeper we go, the bleaker it turns. Our pace is so slow, and my shoes are caving in around my toes. It's the most uncomfortable sensation. The friction burns the skin of my toes and heels. I've never felt such pain.

"What is it?" Lario Exgesis asks. He heard me wince.

"My feet hurt," I grunt. I want to remove the shoes, but I don't want to walk barefoot in the dank mud. Each step brings pure misery, but I grit my teeth and bear it.

Exgesis comes to a stop and kneels on one leg. "Come on, hop on my back."

The discomfort is so severe that I don't hesitate.

I straddle his back, and he easily hoists me securely on top of him. He stands, and I wrap my arms around his neck. After I've safely mounted him, he slides off one shoe and then the other, and he carries them for me.

"Thank you," I reply properly to his sequence of gestures.

"You're welcome," he mumbles.

Off we go, journeying one step at a time. I am not accustomed to traveling at such a slow pace for long journeys. Exgesis doesn't walk us down a clear trail, but he seems sure of every step. It's eerily silent. Neither of us is breathing. The drooping leaves don't rustle or sway. The wind doesn't whistle or howl because, even though the clouds race across the sky, the movement stirs no breeze.

If my senses are correct, we are moving along a decline. I tilt my head back to gaze upward. Thousands of floppy branches twist and turn, wild and out of sorts, encaging us. The way the wood encrusts the bark makes the trees look as if they're wearing faces with drooping eyes, noses, and mouths with lips that zigzag. They are the dreariest trees I've ever seen. They need care and happiness.

I hum the first verse of the Hymn of Gratitude to them. Exgesis turns his head and presses a finger against his lips, urging me to quiet down, but the trees respond. Their stringy limbs sway with the melody. The breeze they conjure cools my damp skin. Instead of quieting down, I increase my volume. All of a sudden, I'm whipped through the air. The wind is almost knocked out of me when Exgesis pins my back against a trunk.

"Be. Silent!" he growls. His teeth are gritted and his jaw clenched.

"I don't understand," I wheeze. What sort of creature has such a hostile reaction to the Hymn of Gratitude? Certainly one who is wicked!

"Two simple things we have to do when going through Rnv: stay quiet and go slow. Simple. Can you do that?"

"But the trees, they welcome the hymn."

Once again, we're staring at each other. For a moment, he looks just as puzzled as I do. Then he laughs—it's a low, guttural sound. It endears him to me and repels simultaneously.

He grunts as he simmers down. He leans his face toward mine to put his mouth close to mine. "You're all wet."

I follow his eyes to the front of my pal'k, wondering what he finds so fascinating. My skin shows through the material that must be wet with sweat. I've never perspired in my whole life. His eyes ravish me; they veer up from between my hips to my breasts until they lock on my eyes. My nakedness has never affected Tryst or any of the mank'-taks like this. I do not understand why I can hardly breathe, why this happens when he regards me in such a way.

"Very nice," he whispers.

I can't say a word. I swallow the knot that has formed in my throat.

"All I can think about is your beautiful body in that dress. I want to throw you down on the ground and…" He releases a brisk breath.

Like he did in my dream? Or was it real? Had he already invaded my mind and my body?

He stares into my eyes. His breaths are heavy. His instrument of sex is firm against the top of my pubic bone, and he's rubbing it up and down against me. I feel something changing inside me. A tingling sensation is forming, and a breath escapes my parted lips.

"Your body responds so easily to this," he whispers.

Suddenly we're pelted by drops of water, and he stops moving his hips. The rain, thick and bulbous, looks like a million diamonds raining on us. This is strange of course, being that the sky is not in view. The water falls straight through the billow of flaccid branches!

The Selell swears and pulls me against him. I twist my neck to look behind us. One drop of water builds upon the last. The rain is rapidly falling, but not a speck of it touches us. Lario Exgesis whips his head around, searching in all directions. He's panicking.

"I told you to stay quiet," he grumbles with his jaw clenched.

The water is taking form, becoming legs, hips, torsos. They have heads now, faces, arms, and all. They surround us. These beings are gigantic and slender. Since they are made of clear liquid, I can see right through them as if I were looking through diamonds.

"Get him!" roars one of the creatures as it aims a long, translucent finger at Lario Exgesis. His voice booms like a thousand drops of water pounding the earth. He speaks in a language I've never heard, but I understand it as if he's spoken in Enuian.

A mountain of water pours over us. Lario Exgesis releases me to throw his hands up in an ill attempt to guard against the tidal wave. I scramble away and turn to see that he's congealed in what looks like a ball of liquid. I cannot believe what I am seeing. He's flinging his arms and kicking, engaged in a desperate struggle to free himself, but even I can see there's no escaping. His movements become slower and slower until he stops, frozen in place.

I have no fear of the translucent creatures. The light within me is taking in their life force, and they are not touched by evil. One of the massive creatures separates from the pack to stand a few feet away from me. A splashing noise resonates as the creature's feet smash against the soil. It's a male. I can tell because of the ripples of muscles in his bare chest and arms. *How can water develop muscle?* I can't stop studying his lofty, translucent toes and fingers. His eyes are blue. I should be shrinking from fear, but I'm not.

"I am Ktkl," he says in his strange tongue.

I'm grateful that he told me his name before I asked. "I am Ad'ru," I say in Enuian.

"You are with the vampire?" His tone is abrasive as he raises his bushy, see-through eyebrows at Lario Exgesis.

I'm caught between concern for Lario Exgesis and being mesmerized by Ktkl, the creature with liquid flesh. "He's my guide. He's helping me find my sister. She's being held captive by the Mtknv."

The creature twists his large neck to look at his companions. He opens his mouth wide and bellows a noise that sounds like a raging waterfall. The others respond likewise. The sound shakes the trees and even the ground.

Ktkl stabs himself in the chest with a long finger. "We Mtknv."

"I don't understand…" I say, although I think I do understand. Lario Exgesis intended to deceive me again. I wonder to what end. "Are you holding a creature like me captive?"

"We hold no lifeblood captive," he declares.

I have no reason to doubt him. He sounds forthright. I point at Exgesis. "But why hold this creature captive?"

"He and the Olligark stole the Scepter of Gant!" the creature roars.

"Then you're familiar with this creature?" I ask in Enuian, affirming what's already been determined.

"I am," Ktkl replies, and he doesn't sound happy about it. He stabs another finger in Lario Exgesis's direction. "We have war because of his crime. Even you are now in danger, Lifeblood. Your worlds are now threatened by the Olligark."

I take a hard look at the Selell, Exgesis. Why are his actions so evil? If we are bonded, then shouldn't he be more of the light and good? His offenses *are* indeed numerous, yet I feel the need to intercede on his behalf. "What are your penalties for his crime?"

"Death," growls Ktkl.

"No." I shake my head. "I cannot let that be. He is my bond. If I live, then he must live."

Ktkl's translucent face grows angrier. Suddenly water rains down on me. It occurs to me that I'm being sentenced for defending Exgesis and declaring that we are bonded. The Mtknv have decided to take me prisoner. But just as fast as the rain falls, the wispy tree branches whip back and forth, generating a forceful wind and making it impossible for the liquid prison to form around me. The wind thrashes every single Mtknv creature. Their liquid composition splashes away, causing them to lose shape. They wail in agony, a sound of destructive rains pounding the earth.

Then it all stops: the rain, the wind, the noise. I'm looking up at the massive, reformed figure that is Ktkl. I feel as if I have swallowed air, but it's still lodged in my throat. We both know what just happened. The trees sided with me. However, they have chosen not to free Lario Exgesis.

"You're free to go," Ktkl says. He sounds as if he's about to take his prisoner and leave.

"Wait, what about my bond?" I cry.

"He stands to face the elder Akltnk."

It almost appears as if Ktkl's large mouth will swallow me whole, but I'm not willing to let my circumstances remain as they are. If they take Exgesis, then I will be alone. *I have never been alone.*

"But he is my companion." I stop short of grabbing Ktkl's powerful liquid arm and pleading for him to release Exgesis.

Ktkl narrows his eyes at me. "Is that what you require? A companion?"

I nod and watch his eyes shift toward the trees to my right. Their branches wave back and forth. I believe Ktkl is communicating with the branches. A gigantic ball of water drops from above. It's another prison, and I recognize the captured. The liquid splashes over the ground, leaving Chex, the Selell, standing not far from me.

"The trees of this region will guide you to your sister," Ktkl says. Again, it appears as if he's readying to leave.

"What about him?" I touch the capsule Lario is stuck in. It feels strange. It's solid, like stone.

"He will stand trial."

"Promise not to pronounce death upon him without my witness?" I ask.

"I cannot make this promise," he replies.

"Then you must kill me too."

"What the hell are you saying?" Chex growls, standing beside me.

I spare him one distracted glance and then a second. Strange—he's not drenched. His clothes and skin are dry. I'm also a little distracted by wondering why he's here in the first place. However, it appears as if my declaration is working. Ktkl is once again conferring with the trees.

"Yes," he grunts, glowering at me. "We will wait for your witness before putting the thief to death. But he is guilty, and he will die."

"All I ask is that you wait," I say over a tiny sigh of relief.

"Open your mouth," Ktkl orders.

I hesitate, but I know the trees will not allow any harm to come to me, and Ktkl is not one who surreptitiously seeks to harm others. I tilt my head back and open my mouth. Ktkl drops a morsel of water on my tongue. I swallow it.

"If you die, I will know, and we will execute him after he is sentenced."

"If I die?" I ask, disturbed by that insinuation. "Do you know what sort of dangers we face?"

"The lifeblood is captive in Siffeo," he grumbles. "You have to cross the Mashlands to enter Siffeo. That may be impossible. But your sister was able to conquer the night spirits."

I catch a cold shiver when he says that.

"And then," he continues, "you will have to conquer the guards of Siffeo. *That* is where the first lifeblood failed."

Before I can respond, the sound of crashing water starts. The Mtknv have collected their catch, and Chex and I watch them disappear beyond the swinging branches, which happen to be my protectors. And the trees are not finished. Where I was once buried beneath their branches that bore down over us, their long, floppy arms are now bent backward to carve a path through the forest. As Ktkl said, they are leading me to my sister.

I put on the tight green shoes and start down the pathway with my scary companion.

CHAPTER 5
BLOWING SMOKE
ADORE

"Well, this is a hell of a situation," Chex complains.

"Why are you here?" I ask, sounding disappointed. I'd hoped he would find his way to Ze Feldis so that Cl'auta could eventually learn I was lost. She would come looking for me and not stop until she found me.

"With the little conscience I have, I couldn't leave you alone with Exgesis," he admits. "You might not get it now, but that guy is certifiable. If those water monsters can kill him, then let them, because we tried and it didn't work."

"They're not monsters. They are creatures." I'm appalled by the way he blatantly links the Mtknv to the evil.

"There's a difference?" He flashes his teeth at me again.

"Yes, there is. One is made by the hand of the evil and the other by the hand of God."

"I guess I'm a monster." He's still grinning, as if such a thing is something that merits great pride.

I take a while to see past the face he's showing. Beyond the surface, there is hopelessness and disappointment.

"Why do you so easily claim the dark and not the light?" I ask. "You were a human before you were a Selell."

His unaffected smile fades into a curious frown. "What the hell is a Selell anyway?"

"Vampyre," I say as if he will understand that terminology.

"You mean *vampire*," he corrects me, emphasizing the long *i* sound.

"Is there a difference?" My tone is slightly harsh because his smile has returned, and I know he's correcting me.

"Didn't you hear it?"

"In pronunciation, but not in definition."

"Ever heard of a homonym?"

"Are you a grammarian?" I ask sharply.

He snorts, and I tear my eyes off that smug

smile of his while wishing it would go away. I feel as if this self-proclaimed monster wants to disturb my el'le'le'kek, my inner peace. We stand facing each other. He is obviously amused by what can be considered an argument between us. I've never engaged in a tiff of this magnitude with anyone other than my sister Na'ta, and I am overwhelmed by the urge to spar with this creature until I become victorious. However, I'm more influenced by the urge to maintain the peace between us. After all, we will be companions until we find Na'ta. Then he will leave this universe since he has no other reason to be here. My sister and I can handle Lario Exgesis and his misfortunes with the Mtknv.

"Do you have your speed, Selell?" I ask, changing the subject.

"Chex is the name, and if you're asking if I can move fast, then the answer is yes."

I can tell that he's bothered by my taciturn tone. "I know your name." As soon as I say it, I wish I hadn't.

Thankfully, Chex doesn't react negatively to my tone this time. He seems to be pondering the fact that I remember his name. I can't help but wonder why it amazes him so.

"We're off to find your sister, yeah?" he asks.

I drop my face to nod, still embarrassed by being so contentious.

"And does she look like you too?"

I lift my head and frown a little. "We favor each other."

"I just want to say, out of all the ones I've seen, you're my favorite." This time when he smiles, it isn't so off-putting.

At first, I'm lost for words. Should I say thank you? Should I ask him to clarify what he means by *favorite*? Instead, I find myself unable to focus on his face. I tear my eyes away from him to glance up the path and then back at him. "We should go."

His habitual smile fades, replaced by a ferocious scowl. It makes me shudder. This Selell clearly means to harm whoever tries to impede our progress.

"After me," he mutters, and without hesitating, he takes off.

We race up the trail the trees have carved out for us, blasting forward at a speed I'm familiar with. The earth hindered me from moving this fast, but not this universe. I feel like we are finally making progress in the search for my sister.

I picture the last time I saw her in my dream. She was in such misery. I'm haunted by how the branches of the wicked tree coiled tightly around her torso, arms, and legs, squeezing her, tormenting her.

Na'ta! I shout within myself, louder than I've ever shouted. I expand my senses, hoping to receive even the tiniest response from her. Optimism eludes me, and rightfully so: I'm still unable to sense her.

This forest is indeed vast. We've traveled a great distance and still have not come to the end of it. I'm happy that the air is no longer stiff, hot, and moist. Ever since the Mtknv arrived, it has cooled down to a tolerable temperature. The trees are kinder to us and have stirred up a light, inviting breeze. But I am perspiring again, and I'm suddenly self-conscious about it. I glance at Chex. He's observing me.

"What is it?" I anxiously ask.

He's not devouring me with his eyes, and I am relieved. Although I wonder—if he did watch me in that way, would it have the same effect on me?

"Where are you from?" he asks, interrupting my train of thought. The look on his face tells me that he's extremely interested in my answer.

"I am from Enu."

"Right. I can smell that you're not human, but where on *Earth* are you from? You have a life on Earth, don't you?"

"No. I'd never been there until…" I'm suddenly struck by what lies before us.

We come to an abrupt stop because we have reached the edge of the forest. My lips part in awe, and so do Chex's. The land ahead of us is like a sheet of smooth stone, but it's dry and has millions of deep, narrow cracks. The plane is barren, holding no plant life, and I venture to say that no living species could seek to survive here. As I gaze farther out in the distance, I see pockets of smoke rising behind the flat-topped mountain range that stretches farther than our eyes can see.

For the life of me, my eyes seek the sun. There it is, red and ominous. It looks as if it has been stabbed in the heart and is bleeding to death. I feel as though my majestic Enu was merely a place I lived once upon a time in a wonderful dream.

"What the hell?" Chex marvels at the spectacle before us. He looks down to examine the dry earth that's only one step away.

He carefully presses a foot against the dry ground. I gasp when I see it go right through.

"See this? These Mash monsters"—he glances at me—"creatures, whatever the hell you want to call them, have come to play." He hawks out into the distance with his eyes narrowed and top lip curled.

"It's a trap," I say, stating the obvious. However, I'm compelled to test the ground with my own foot.

Chex and I look at each other, dumbfounded. My foot doesn't sink through.

Suddenly, he becomes very still. "Do you hear that?" He takes care to whisper.

I open my ears. "Just the breeze behind us."

"No, that's not it. How good are you in a fight? Are you anything like your sister Glo?" he asks in a rush.

"Well, no," I reply, feeling as though I've disappointed him. "Glo's power is of the body. Mine is of the mind..." My words trail off, and I gulp at what I see.

A black swarm rises out of the mountain range and momentarily hovers above it. The creatures have fluttering wings, and they know exactly where we stand.

"Are those bats?" I ask, spellbound by the sight of them.

"No."

"Then what are they?" I whisper, not expecting Chex to know the answer.

Their wings are spiny and flapping rapidly as they soar in our direction. I'm petrified.

"Hell if I know, but if you can't fight, then get back in the woods!" he shouts above their buzzing noise.

I turn to look behind me. There lies the safety of the forest. The trees have kept me from being imprisoned by the Mtknv, and I'm sure they'll keep me from being devoured by the Mash. But the Selell is standing bravely beside me. He's willing to fight, and for what? *My* sister's freedom? He has loyalties and allegiances, if not to me, then certainly to Baron Ze Feldis. But he doesn't run and hide in the forest. Yet here I stand, considering doing just that.

The creatures are closer and the noise louder. Their refrain is a combination of buzzing and growling. Now I can see that they're not bats. They have bony arms and legs and long feet with broad heels. They are black and chalky looking. As they squawk, they open their mouths wide, revealing sharp teeth.

I let out a long breath once I realize I've been holding it. "I'll stay."

"If you're going to die, go. If you're going to live, then stay," the Selell shouts.

"I'll live!" But I am terrified. Is this the sort of peril my sisters have faced and I have avoided throughout the centuries?

"Rule number one: never let him hit first!" Chex shouts in my ear.

He takes a huge leap toward the desert land and hovers above the ground. There are hundreds of them and one of him, yet he's streaking ahead like the numbers are in his favor.

I can't let him leap alone. I summon the power of light to my hands, all of it. Every fiber of my being dreads getting close to those creatures, but I charge forward, staying as close to Chex as I can. Black ashes spray over me as he clashes with the first flank of Mash creatures, and I lose sight of him. Grit pours in my eyes and up my nose. I'm coughing, trying to stop myself from suffocating. All I see is black. I feel the creatures press against my chest, both sides of my head, and my body. At first I'm befuddled because I've never been this close to losing my life, but an instinct to survive grips me. I gain control of my mind and tell the light that I want these creatures to release me and I want them gone.

Power pours out of my skin like a geyser. Waves of powdery ash explode all around me. The light doesn't simmer—it intensifies, following the command of my will. My arms swing in every direction. The light stabs the creatures before they can get near me, and they explode into black particles. Their screams turn more abrasive. Those that remain alive retreat to the mountains, which suck them in.

Silence prevails. It's still again. Chex and I are alone, hovering above the deserted land below.

I'm still jittery. I look down at myself all soiled by grime then over at Chex. He doesn't have a speck of ash on him. I'm praying they don't come back. I don't ever want to see them again.

"Are you all right?" Chex asks, studying me with deep concern.

I'm holding myself and shaking. I shut my eyes tight and force myself to stop shivering. It takes a few moments, but I stop. "Yes. But why are you not soiled?" Sometimes I'm surprised by my own curiosity.

"Because I'm an artist, darling," he mumbles, taking me seriously as he stares into the distance. He inhales deeply and slowly, carefully releasing the air out through his nostrils. "I don't know what we're in for, but whatever you just did, keep it up. And your sister is out there." He glances at me. "I can smell her."

"You can?" I'm surprised. "Then why can't I sense her?" I mumble to myself.

Rightfully, Chex doesn't answer. He's quite intuitive. Instead he says, "Let's go," and starts toward the mountains.

Once again, I follow where he leads. We're standing in a field of grass that's so coarse and high, the blades pinch my bare arms and legs and scratch my cheeks. A white, smoky haze settles all around us. The mist is a mixture of low-hanging cumulus clouds and settling smoke from the raging fire pits that are plopped throughout the field. I'm skittish because I thought I saw something peculiar as we made our descent into the grass.

"One second," Chex says. His ears and eyes are on alert. He inhales deeply.

I tug at the ends of my hair, lifting it off my neck. It doesn't help. The heat is still torturing me.

"What is it?" he asks, frowning at me.

"I'm uncomfortable." I'm still holding my hair above my neck, but it only gives me a little reprieve.

Suddenly Chex is behind me, and my hair is tightly pulled at the back of my head. I reach around to touch it.

"Oh." I pull a long braid forward and lay it across my shoulder. "Thanks." I'm surprised that he committed this act of kindness toward me.

"You're welcome." He displays that toothy smile of his.

I'm processing how differently I feel about that expression when flames ignite beneath our feet. "Up!" I shout and wrap my fingers around Chex's wrists.

He swiftly changes the position of our hands and pulls me into the clouds. We hover over the area we just escaped. Orange flames soar, crackle, and pop where we last stood. That's exactly what I suspected when we first landed in the field—the bowls of fire are not static. The blaze beneath us explodes, shooting flames high into the clouds. I watch the molten heat heading for us. There's no way we can escape. Then all of a sudden, I'm bolting across the atmosphere above the field, pulled along by Chex. Pits of fire ignite beneath us, chasing us until we clear the wild meadow.

Soon we're standing on a narrow, dusty road that cuts between two clay walls of structures that look like the abandoned ruins of the earth's ancient Mayans. As we stand in the open, I finally feel Na'ta. She's like the warmth of home flooding my insides. Our souls connect, and all I feel is the path that guides me to her.

I leap off the ground to allow my body to carry me to her, but I slam right into Chex's chest. He grasps my shoulders to hold me still, and then in a flash, he has me hemmed up against the wall in a tight, dark corner.

"Where the hell do you think you're going?" he whispers. His very strange and unnatural black eyes shine in the shadowy crevice.

I fidget against his firm grasp. "Na'ta, she's here!"

"Quiet," he warns me. "Do you *think* whatever the hell's been trying to kill us has given up because you've got a line on your sister?"

"I came here to get my sister." I jab him in the chest with my hands, attempting to push him out of my way, but he's unyielding, like a boulder.

"Keep. Your. Voice. Down," he scolds me in a whisper. His black eyes gaze deeply into mine. Then he dips his face forward to position his nose between my lips. He takes a long, indulgent inale and then closes his eyes to savor my scent. "I'll follow that."

I can't move and can barely breathe. My eyes are focused on the sharp angles of his face. I believe he said, "I'll follow that," but I'm not sure. I am mesmerized. Oh my, has this Selell bewitched me? "What did you say?" I breathe.

"Don't move."

"But…"

"Stay here," he softly demands.

I feel my eyebrows pull toward the bridge of my nose, but I acquiesce by nodding. He's gone. I'm alone in the crevice. Every cell of my body feels constricted, and while I wait for this feeling to free me, a loud chirp, like a very huge bird, echoes in the distance, then another and another. The sound continues, but never more than one chirp at a time. It makes me nervous. Chex has been gone longer than I'm comfortable with.

I hear *plop, plop, plop*… I stifle a gasp. Whatever or whoever is making that sound is near. I press my back closer to the wall, hoping the dark shadows will conceal me. Anticipation squeezes me so tightly that I feel I might pass out. I hear the being lurking, and its breaths are husky, as if it's straining to cycle the opaque air. Beyond the shadows, the first part of a leg becomes visible. It's a bony limb with a hoofed foot, the leg of a stallion. I'm both eager and frightened to see the rest of the creature, and I don't have to wait long. There it is, not far away from my hiding place.

The creature's two legs, feet, groin, buttocks, torso, and chest are those of a brown mare. Its shoulders, arms, face, and neck closely resemble a human's, but these parts lack flesh and bone. Instead, they're composed of vapor, maybe smoke, and when it breathes, a ball of fire shoots out of its mouth and dissipates into thin air.

The creature is searching along the block walls and in every corner. I stay still. Since I don't need to breathe to survive, I stop breathing. Worry sets in. What will happen to me when it sees me? I don't have to wait another second to find out.

The creature shifts its smoky head to the right and faces me. I'm stunned as it opens its mouth and lets out a loud chirp. I wait to hear the answering chirp, but the call isn't returned. At first, the creature twitches its neck a little. Its face looks confused and then angry as it leans into me with rage in its eyes.

I don't hesitate to lift my palms and release the i'lek'u. The light stabs it in the heart. Instantly, the creature softens its infuriated face. I'm relieved to breathe again as we stand, observing each other.

"What are you?" I ask while watching its slightest movements.

"A guard of Siffeo," it says morosely, watching me.

I wonder if it's waiting to take instruction from me. "Will you let me go if I request it?" I ask, testing my assumption.

Before the creature can answer, in a blink of my eyes, it's laid out on the grimy ground, smoke pouring from a hole in its chest.

Chex is back and standing in front of me. He stuffs a dagger into the lining of his black duster coat. "Simple." He looks down at his victim.

"Did you just kill it?" I ask, flabbergasted. He didn't have to do that. The creature was under the influence of the light. It wasn't going to hurt me or Chex.

He shrugs, nonchalant about the slaying. "You'll want him dead when you see what he's done to your sister."

Suddenly, my heart is full of hope. "You've seen her?"

"I did," he says with a smug lift of his top lip. "I took out the croakers with the foggy heads but…" He snorts. "It won't be a cakewalk getting to her."

"Cakewalk?" I ask, confused.

"Just a figure of speech. Come on."

He takes off down the alley, and I follow. When I turn back for one final glance at the dead creature, it's consumed by fire. My heart breaks for it as I continue across the dusty path. I cannot properly mourn it. Na'ta's distress presses upon me. Saving her is all I can focus on. Chex's pace is swift, but he's smooth, a master of riding the wind. He's like a soft breeze, but also a violent storm. This is evident in the blistering balls of fire we pass over.

"Did you have to kill them all?" I ask, bewildered by the sight of more death.

"Yes," he replies, sharply and without remorse.

The farther we voyage into Siffeo, the more pockets of writhing flames we pass over. The scenery doesn't change until we reach a wide doorway. Beyond it is pitch black. But we don't enter—we continue on, up and down the alleys, passing more entries. I feel as if we're moving in circles, yet Na'ta is closer. I reach out for her. I'm consumed by relief when I feel her weak pulse and fading heartbeat.

Adore, is it you? she whimpers to me.

I'm here. I don't want to see the endless rows of gray mortar; I want to see *her*. As my impatience grows, we come to an abrupt stop. Chex takes me once again and shoves me into another dark corner.

"If you are afraid, then kill it right here and now," he mutters. His bottomless eyes are staring into mine. "We're not going to win this if you're scared."

I gulp, transfixed by his eyes, even at a time like this. "Is that how you're able to do it so easily?"

His eyes expand, and he puts his face a hair closer to mine. "You want to live?"

"Yes," I croak.

"You see how close we are to your sister? Do you think we could've gotten here diplomatically?"

My mind flashes pictures of the black creatures that attacked us from the depths of the mountains bordering the Mashlands, being chased by the live fire in the fields outside this desolate maze, and then coming face to face with a guard of Siffeo. If it weren't for the light, he would've captured me, and maybe I would have met Na'ta's fate.

"No," I conclude.

He blinks, shocked by my response. "Right." He smirks, not showing teeth. "Then let's go get them." Now he shows teeth.

Chex steps out of the corner and into plain sight. He stands still, waiting for me to take my place at his side. I don't have to heed his warning and kill my fear because I have none. I only have drive. I will do whatever it takes to relieve Na'ta's angst. As a daughter of The House of Benel, it is my duty.

I join him. He examines me to assess my resolve. I show him what he's seeking. No longer doubtful, we streak forward. I know exactly where to go. Na'ta is strong within me. Feeling her distress makes my nostrils swell and my eyes well up with tears. My emotions are heightened. This is new to me. Could this be rage? Vengeance?

Together, we streak through one of the broad entryways and are high up in a red sky. It is hotter here than any place I have been since being lured out of Enu, but Chex doesn't stop to take in the ambiance. I'm a step behind him as he streaks toward an enormous cone-shaped configuration, billows of fire swelling from its top. It's not a mountain, although it resembles one in height and mass; it's made of a solid red stone that resembles a massive ruby. Creatures that look like the guards of Siffeo prance and gallop around it with stallion-like legs, performing some sort of shuffling dance.

The creatures are too preoccupied with what they are doing to notice us. I wonder what they would do if they saw us. Would they attack? It almost looks like Chex is going to lead us right into their midst, but he makes a sharp turn toward a low valley that holds the desolate forest of dead trees I saw in my dream. The wild, leafless branches stick straight out from the bark like a sea of spiky, sharp spears.

"There she is!" I cry.

It's Na'ta! My heart sinks when I see her. She's positioned upside down, and her long black hair is dusty from sweeping the dirty ground. One branch has punctured her black shirt and gone clean through her heart and out of her back. Another branch stabs her through one thigh and a third branch through the other thigh.

"Shit!" Chex shouts. "Already?"

I look up to see what he's referring to. I can't count the number of guards of Siffeo that are shooting into the space above us through the doorway we entered, but there are many of them. I wonder if they rose to life from the fiery mess Chex left them in. They hover, searching for the trespassers. Their chirping is so loud, it's like being gouged in the ears by a spear-tipped branch. I glance toward the creatures dancing around the pillar. I hope they don't decide to join those hovering above us, exponentially increasing their numbers. What's strange is that they don't even acknowledge the flanks growing in the sky. They continue galloping and prancing and turning and bowing.

Balls of fire are unleashed on us. It's time to fight, so I lift my palms and send my light to clash with their fire. The creatures screech as the flames wither into smoke. They are inherently connected to their fire like I am to my light.

"Get her!" Chex shouts, motioning toward Na'ta. "And I'll get them!" With that said, he blazes up.

He's so fast that my eyes lose track of him, but creatures are falling all around me, going down in puffs of smoke. They seem not to focus on me as they try to locate Chex and stop him from picking them off in droves. Chex—what sort of Selell is he that he can kill so expertly?

But this gives me the opportunity to focus fully on freeing Na'ta. The tree that holds her captive has caught fire. I run as fast as I can to free her. When I reach her, I kneel to put my face close to hers. "Na'ta…"

Her eyes are wide open, but she looks dead already. I'm hit by a ball of fire. I feel a temporary burning sensation before it extinguishes against my skin. The pal'k I'm wearing doesn't go up in flames. I must be untouchable by their weapons and so is Na'ta, which may be the reason she's still alive.

But I look down at my ankles because something has just wrapped around them and is squeezing tightly. It's a branch from the same tree. I clamp my hands around it and douse it with the light. It quickly uncoils and squeals as it retreats.

My light is the answer.

I press my hands against Na'ta's cheek and fill her with it. Soon she glows like the perfect sun, and the branches that pierce her withdraw. I catch her before she hits the ground, and I cradle her in my arms.

"Na'ta," I say, smoothing her hair from her face.

She answers me by gazing deeply into my eyes before closing hers. She's sleeping, aware that I have her. Now we must escape. I'm sure we can take cover in the forest from which we came. The trees have proven to be my ally.

I look up to search for the way out. The sky is flooded with the guards of Siffeo. There are too many of them. It seems just as Chex sends one to the ground, another one appears. It would be impossible to break their flanks and get out unscathed. But I must.

In my arms, Na'ta's limp body is as light as a puek leaf. I make sure she's secure in my grasp as I push up toward the way out. I'm quick but not fast enough. I come to an abrupt stop as four pairs of hooves prepare to clomp me back down to the hazardous forest. But suddenly—almost simultane-ously—the hooves free-fall.

"Go! Don't stop!" Chex shouts as he swoops past me so fast that he's a blur.

He sounds confident in my ability to make it out of here. I drink in his certainty as I focus on the light that outlines the portal. More sets of hooves threaten to stop me, but I don't let them spook me or deter my progress.

I go, and I go, and I go until I'm back under a smoky night sky and trapped between the walls of the ruins. It appears that we're alone, but I know better than to stop and enjoy the false sense of relief. They're here. I can feel them. I increase my pace as I walk the wind, lifting way above this Potemkin village, and head toward the mountains where the Mash creatures flap above the range. I'm still determined not to stop. Way in the distance, the kark trees are a welcoming sight. I can almost hear them calling us to them.

"We're almost there, Na'ta," I whisper as I streak straight ahead.

Suddenly, I'm caught in a swarm of blackness. Panic sets in. I use all of my strength to hold Na'ta closer. I'll die before I drop her. I'm waiting to be smothered by them like before, but instead, I'm drenched with water, and the darkness fades. The sound of water crashing against the arid surface below is deafening. It's raining hard, and I'm holding up in the downpour.

When it finally stops, the ash creatures are mud. The water lifts off the surface and forms into Ktkl, who stands right in front of me. About twenty other Mtknv creatures surround us, fencing us in. Before I'm able to thank Ktkl for rescuing us, more water gushes over me, and I'm trapped in my own bulbous prison while still cradling Na'ta.

CHAPTER 6
THE FIRST TOUCH
ADORE

I am confused about why Ktkl would imprison me. Have I committed a crime against the Mtknv? I try to shift, but the liquid is unyielding.

"To the kark," Na'ta says in a weak voice.

Her trapped body shivers against me, and panic starts to rule my reasoning. Chex appears outside our bubble, and I see Ktkl glaring at him. Water pours down over Chex, but he's already gone, evading the prison.

It is time for me to summon the light. When I do, it willingly obeys. The substance that entraps me is set alight and gets brighter and brighter. The solid compound turns to liquid and splashes to the ground. We're free. The kark trees are not far, and I take off like Na'ta's life depends on it.

The sound of crashing water chases me, but I will not be stopped. As soon as I enter the forest, the floppy branches pull Na'ta out of my arms, and I come to an abrupt stop. My heart is pounding. I watch the strappy branches roll her deep into them until she's curled up and fastened against the trunk of a tree. But they're not done. A long twig snakes toward Na'ta's mouth and slides between her lips. It appears the trees are nourishing her.

"That a good thing?" Chex asks as he appears at my side, squinting at my sister.

"Yes, I think it is." I sigh with relief. The normal blush in her cheeks is already returning. "But I don't understand why Ktkl would attack us."

"Trust no one, and then you won't be surprised."

I ponder his words. Surely he can't distrust every creature, not after all we've been through together in this short period of time.

"What about me?" I'm forced to ask him. "Do you trust me?"

"No," he says.

"But why not?" I can't mask the disappointment in my voice.

As I wait for his reply, there's a loud splash behind us. We turn to find Ktkl, his face contorted in anger. He happens to be alone.

"Where is the vampire?" he roars so loudly that the tree leaves shake.

I widen my eyes at Chex because I'm confused. Which Selell could he be referring to? Na'ta often travels with the Selell Telman, but he's not present. Could he have committed offenses against the Mtknv too? Has Na'ta gotten herself into trouble with another species, as she often does?

"He means Exgesis," Chex mutters. "He must've given them the shake. He's a slippery bastard."

"Is that true?" I ask Ktkl.

"Yes. True." His anger subsides a little. "You did not help him?"

"Absolutely not!" I glance at Na'ta in the safety of the tree. "I told you that my priority was finding my sister."

"He freed himself, just as you released yourself."

"He used the light?" I ask, sort of shocked.

"Yes, he did."

"*Se'im El'ko te*," I whisper gravely and touch my heart. I'm stunned. "He has the same powers I have because we're bonded."

"No way!" Chex shouts.

"But where did he go? Why didn't he come back to help us?" I can't believe it. I thought he was supposed to help me find my sister. He gave me his word.

Chex snorts. "You really are quite new, aren't you?"

I shake my head. "I don't understand what you mean."

"Listen, Ad'ru? Right?"

"If you're asking if my name is Ad'ru, then yes." I thought he knew my given name. I don't understand why this is so, but I'm disappointed he had to ask.

"Exgesis was never on your side. The only side he's ever been on is his own. He wants something from you, and I don't think you gave it to him—not yet." Chex takes a thoughtful pause. "The only question is why did he want you to come here with him? And where the hell is he?"

I sigh, frustrated, because I have no answers. My heart sinks. It becomes apparent to me that I cannot return to Enu as long as Lario Exgesis remains my bond. Now that I've stepped foot on the earth, if I go home, he will have my full capabilities. I cannot unleash such a being on any world. So I set my jaw. "I'll find him. And he will face your justice."

Ktkl's powerful face moves through a series of expressions as he ponders my words. He tilts his massive head back to look at Na'ta. "I accept your vow."

"Thank you," I say sincerely.

Ktkl bursts into billions of tiny drops of water. I watch in awe as each drop is sucked into one of the bulbous cumulus clouds racing across the murky sky. I turn to look up at Chex because I can feel him staring at me.

"You know what?" he asks.

"What?" I barely say as I touch where my heart resides. This Selell should not have the ability to make my heart jump in such a manner.

"I take it back. I trust you." He winks at me with a smile, an actual, genuine, warm-hearted smile.

"That makes me happy." I feel the glee in my grin.

"Good." He lifts his eyebrows. "Because you're the first person I ever said that to and meant it."

We stare at each other in silence. I feel as if we should kiss or something, but that would not be appropriate. So I rip my eyes away from his face to study Na'ta in the tree. We can't leave until she is better. We have to wait it out, and I've never felt so grimy in my life. I look at my dress, which is no longer free of stains—it has been soiled by ash, dust, smudges of wild grass, and even my own sweat. It is no longer wearable.

"You want to get clean?" Chex asks while observing me observe myself.

"Yes." I take my dress hem and lift it, but I only get as far as my upper thigh before he grabs my wrists.

"Whoa! You can't do that!"

"But I can't keep it on. It's tarnished," I complain.

"You can't get naked either. I'm a vampire, but I'm still a man, you know?"

"No. I don't understand." I frown at him, confused and slightly agitated by how tightly he's holding my wrists. "Can you let go of me please?"

"Only if you promise not to take your clothes off."

I sigh hard. I didn't think Selells had an issue with nudity. Certainly my sisters' bonds have no issue with theirs or mine. "I promise." By no means do I want to make him uncomfortable.

He removes his hands but keeps his eyes pinned

to my hips for a few moments before putting them back on my face. "Follow me."

I hesitate because I don't want to go where Na'ta is out of my sight.

"She'll be fine." He sounds sure of that. He even holds out his hand for me to take.

It's such an inviting gesture from one so austere that I can't help but rest my palm on top of his.

He gazes at my fingers. "Ah," he breathes softly. "Still so new."

Before I can ask what he means by "new," he whisks me away. We sweep past hefty, aged kark trees as we journey deeper into the dark forest. Chex seems to know his way around. I'm wondering about that when there's an abrupt change of scenery. We're standing at the edge of a natural pool of bubbling clear water.

I'm so excited to see it that I squeeze his shoulder. "How did you find this?"

"I found it before the water creatures found me."

I smile at him because he called the Mtknv *creatures* and not monsters. All of a sudden, we're once again locked in each other's gaze. What's happening to me? First it was Lario Exgesis who made me feel this way, and there was a good reason for it. We are bonded. I cannot be bonded to Chex as well. Yet his touch, his smile, even the wicked one, and his voice make my stomach flutter.

"Well," he says, "I'll leave you to it."

"No way." I grab *his* arm this time. "You must join me."

He shakes his head and steps away from me. "You don't know what you're asking."

"Yes, I do. I don't mind the nakedness. Where I'm from, we primarily do not wear garments." I feel the need to explain.

"Or panties," he mutters with his eyes fastened on my groin.

"No," I timidly reply as I remember what *panties* are. I have never worn them, but I do know they are Earth garments. The bigger problem is that I cannot bathe alone because I don't like being by myself, and his companionship is beyond sufficient. "But I'm fine with it. I swim naked with Tryst all the time."

"Who the hell is Tryst?" he says with a laugh.

"He's my friend…" The amusement in his expression makes me pause. "At home." I don't think Chex takes me seriously much. I'm beginning to understand what he means by "new." However, he must understand that he's new to me too.

"You know what? What the hell," he says to my surprise. He slips off his jacket and then the soft gray shirt he's wearing beneath it.

I am in awe of his broad shoulders and the ripples of muscles that cross his chest, which starts wide at the top but tapers toward his waist. In his physique lies the pure definition of strength, and apparently my eyes, and other parts of me, find him attractive. He hasn't given me permission, but it's too late. My fingers ride across his skin. He has a solid structure, but he's lukewarm. Yet I don't find his temperature repellant.

"What the hell?" he mutters as he flinches in surprise.

He's reacting to the i'lek'u that sparkles in my eyes. I too am shocked by my reaction to him. This has never happened to me. In embarrassment, I drop my face to study the solid stone beneath my feet. But he puts a finger under my chin and lifts my face. His mouth is caught open, and he's staring at me. Only now do I realize what I've done.

"I apologize," I say as I gently remove his hand from my face.

"For what?" he breathlessly asks.

"I was rude. I violated your being."

He frowns thoughtfully. "I can't believe you touched me. I never let anyone touch me like that."

I shake my head as my shame deepens. "I'm so sorry."

"Don't." He softly swipes the back of his strong hand down my cheek. "You can't know what you're doing to me. You're too new to know."

"Then you forgive me?" I feel hope in my eyes.

He steps closer. "There's nothing to forgive."

I gulp. "It's our custom to ask if we're seeking amusement or pleasure by touching a strange being."

"That's a custom?" He narrows his eyes. "And I'm *strange*?"

"You're new to me too," I say with a smile. I'm happy the opportunity arose where I could convey that thought to him.

Chex releases a sweet, jovial laugh. "Only if the shitload of my enemies can see me now. Get clean." He's still laughing while thumbing over his shoulder, "I'm going to find my own watering hole, because I want *you* to give *me* permission to violate you too."

"Oh, you can touch me!" I gladly slip out of my pal'k and toss it into the pool of water.

His laughing comes to an immediate stop. I've angered him. I see that by the look on his face. But then his eyes fall over my breasts and down my sternum to my pelvis. I see that he wants to touch me, explore who I am as I desire to explore who he is.

"It's okay," I say breathlessly, trying to constrain my strong urge to experience his hands on my body.

He pauses, deliberating, I presume. He moves closer and slides his fingers between my thighs. I inhale sharply, and so does he as I look to see his hand massaging my flesh. His hand goes higher and higher until he touches my genitals. He kneads the human point of my body called a clitoris, and a strange sensation gradually overtakes me. It's like the hum of the *ak'arunu*, an instrument that resembles a flute.

"Is this what you're inviting me to do to you?" His voice is husky and seductive.

I can't speak because the song he's playing is growing louder. A moan escapes me. "What are you doing?" I'm finally able to whisper.

"I'm making you come."

"But I'm already here?" I find myself whimpering.

He flashes a smoldering grin. "What are you feeling, Ad'ru?"

What am I feeling? I feel weak in the knees, and

I need to hold on to something or I'll sink into the earth. What do I feel? "Pleasure."

"Do you want me to stop?"

I feel his cold breath sweep across the very tip of my receptive nipple. But his face—I can't see it because my eyelids have fluttered closed. They're still heavy, but I lift them as high as I can. That's when I see that his top lip is curled and stretched over his two pronounced canine teeth.

"Yes, stop," I gasp, no longer under seduction's spell. I watch his fangs slowly retract. His fingers, his instruments of pleasure, abandon me, but he still holds me close.

"Are you afraid of me, Ad'ru?" he whispers.

I want to say no, but instead, I tell him the truth. "I'm afraid of what you are able to do to me."

He tilts his head as he searches my face for meaning. Funny, he doesn't realize that I'm afraid of the mere essence of what he is—a Selell who, upon the earth, thirsts for blood. In that universe, consuming every drop of my blood can give him unimaginable power, and when I'm drained of my lifeblood, I will die.

"You should get cleaned up," he says as he lets go of me. There's a change in his tone. His passion has subsided, and I already miss his touch and nearness.

"Are you leaving?" I ask as a sudden feeling of impending loneliness creeps up on me.

"Hell no," he says emphatically. "I'm dirty too."

"So you'll bathe with me?"

He lifts one side of his mouth again, showing me a flash of teeth. "Get in." He nudges his chin toward the bubbling water.

I'm relieved that he will stay. Standing on the edge of the pool, I leap and curl backward, diving into the water. The pool is not very deep. I swim approximately ten feet below the surface before my hands touch the bedrock. I'm surprised by how warm and soft the water is as I head back to the top. When my head emerges, the first thing I see is Chex standing at the ledge of the pond. He's completely naked, and I can't take my eyes off his male organ. It's long and erect, and he watches me observe it.

What an interesting sight. Tryst doesn't have one. The Selell Lario Exgesis had one. I felt it against me whenever he held me close, but I never saw it like that. I do want to touch Chex's, but his two canine teeth once again touch his lower lip.

"Don't worry, darling; no means no," he says. In an instant, he's in the pool beside me.

As we study each other, I feel the giddy feeling I get whenever I'm aware that he's this close.

"So what's all this bonding shit about?" he asks, leaning in slightly closer.

When I become aware that I too am inclining toward him, I stop myself, swallow the lump in my throat, and say in an unnaturally high voice, "We, the daughters of the House of Benel, are bonded to Selells."

He's slowly swiping his arms back and forth, treading water. "Selells... Why vampires? Why not a less brutal creature?"

"Out of all the creatures on Earth contained in flesh, you are the least brutal."

"Ha! And why is that?" There's vulnerability in his curiosity.

"Because your days have been longer and that has made you wiser," I reply, paraphrasing a key point my father once taught me.

After one burst of movement, his arms are wrapped around me. His hands are at the bottom of my back, holding me close to his firm exterior. "Do you know what it is to live for centuries, thirsting for blood and not having it because no human in their right mind will give it to you? I don't know where you got your intelligence from, but you might want to regard my species as the most brutal blokes you'll encounter in every shitty universe in existence. You want to know why?" My lips part as I think of an answer, but he says, "Because we're desperate, Ad'ru. We're thirsty. All the damn time."

Multiple thoughts compete with each other in my head, and the one that's tethered to the desires brewing deep inside me win.

"Are you thirsty now?" I barely mutter, unable to look away from his pulsating fangs.

He slowly shakes his head. "Not recently."

"So you're not thirsty for my blood?"

He touches one of his sharp teeth. "You're talking about these?"

I nod stiffly. Since I'm finding it difficult to breathe, I stop doing it altogether.

"These are *bonded* to this." He thrusts his hand under the water and pushes his firm organ against my pelvic bone.

Once again, I'm hosting a multitude of thoughts.

"Why are you frowning?" Chex whispers,

breaking my concentration. "What are you thinking?"

Du, or for one, I'm thinking how he and I are definitely bonded, even if it's not in accordance with the Pact of Gogulon. His loyalty and the way I trust him unites us. *Dut,* or secondly, I wonder why his man part grows so rigid when his fangs throb like that? If he's not thirsty for my lifeblood, then what does he crave so powerfully? These thoughts are strong, but one is more stalwart than the others.

"Well," I say timidly, "I wonder what you're supposed to do with that." I point beneath the water.

He unleashes a booming laugh, one that echoes throughout the forest. "You're way too sexy to have to ask that question!" He grabs me again, which is an act he does so freely. "You're beautiful as hell, but I've never given a shit about that. Like you said, a vampire lives a long time, and I've been in this godforsaken body for centuries. Beautiful women are as abundant as flies on shit." Then he narrows his eyes and gazes deeply into mine. I'm immobilized by his embrace and powerfully hypnotic glare. He continues, "It's all that you are, Ad'ru. I don't want to fuck you. You make me want to put in the work it'll take to make love to you." He sips air between his teeth as he closes his eyes. "It's torture to know that Exgesis gets to have you like Ze Feldis, Elo, and Askin get to have your sisters."

My pulse races. Especially since I think I understand what he's trying to convey. "So you would use that on me, like my sisters' bonds use it on them. Sex?" I gasp at the revelation. Sex! That's what he wants to engage in with me. "You lust after me?"

He grins at me, and I sense he's amused by my inquiry. "You can say that."

"Hey, Adore," a familiar and lackluster voice says from behind Chex.

I jump, startled. I curve around his towering physique to see Na'ta standing at the edge of the pool. My thoughts are once again split. Chex's last reply still turns in my head, but I'm excited to finally see my sister standing strong.

"You look well," I say to her.

She lifts her eyebrows suspiciously at Chex. "I see you're becoming acquainted with the ways of man." She's being cynical, of course, which is the natural way of Na'ta.

"To be continued," Chex whispers as he slides a finger up my clitoris.

I have an automatic response to the sensation.

"Adore!" Na'ta barks. "Get out of the water!" She scowls at Chex, who's glaring at her with that toothy smile.

I'm still slightly dazed, but I swim over to the edge of the pool and lift myself out of it.

"You're dripping wet," Na'ta observes with her nose crinkled. But she still embraces me and kisses me on the cheek. "I was so damn glad to see you." She squeezes me tightly.

"I'm glad to see you too." I sigh. However, I'm also a little miffed that she's here at all! I want to ask her why she came to this universe in the first place.

But Na'ta is quick in all things. Her demeanor changes when she releases me and looks past me. "Is he your Selell?"

I turn to glance at him. He seems very distracted by my nakedness although he is making an attempt to follow our conversation.

"No," I sadly answer.

Na'ta nods once. She has a pragmatic expression. History has taught me that that look means she's conjuring a plan that usually involves the threat of death or injury.

"That's too bad," she mutters, looking far off. "We could've used your bond to easily open the gate to Tetra. The combined power of the i'lek'u will open it in a jiffy."

"Tetra?" I blurt before she can continue.

"Adore, behind the gates are the souls of Selells who are dead," she says as if I do not already know this. "We have to get Telman out of there. He's still of flesh and here, beyond the earth, breath. The souls can kill him, and he'll be lost to me forever." She's flustered by the time she finishes.

"Give me five seconds," Chex says.

In less than that time, he's standing next to me, clothed and holding my wet pal'k.

"She can't wear that," Na'ta says as she reaches to swipe the garment out of his hands.

"Hey! Manners!" Chex gripes as he pulls it back before she can snatch it. He puts it securely into my hand.

Na'ta snorts, slighted because, in her mind, he just won. That's how Na'ta thinks. She has to get her way to be victorious.

"You sure this one isn't your bond?" She sneers at him. "Since he so easily inserts himself into family matters."

"Not families, just Ad'ru's," Chex snaps. Just as I knew he would. He's not one to spurn confrontation, and neither is she.

"Oh," Na'ta cynically sings as she carefully takes the pal'k from me. "You speak Enuian, I see." She curls her top lip. "Ne'lek' Ad'ru ne'tekk'ta lep'ot."

Chex takes his hardened gaze off of her and looks to me for interpretation.

"She said that you only want to see me naked and wet."

He lifts his eyebrows and grunts, vaguely amused by that.

"Plus where we're going, you can't wear this." She shakes the pal'k.

"Where are we going?" I ask warily.

She points her chin at Chex. "He's going to have to do. It would be nice to have the Selell with the light to get us in, but I think a few drops of his blood will open the door."

"My blood?" Chex exclaims. "No one takes my blood. Not even her." He stabs his thumb in my direction.

"I'll be back," Na'ta says, ignoring his protestation. Faster than instantly, she's gone.

Chex blinks as if his eyes deceived him. "Did she just disappear?"

I shake my head. "No, she holds the power of speed. She's moving through space, but at a speed no creature other than the Creator himself can travel."

He flinches, taken aback. "God? You believe in that shit?" He narrows his eyes to slits as he studies me.

I can tell he's searching for something in my expression, and I have no idea what that is. I hesitate even though I have a concise answer to his unexpected question. "I have no beliefs."

His stare grows more intense. I've seen that look on all of my sisters' faces when they were introduced to Enu and their plight for the first time. He cannot comprehend what I have said.

"Should I explain?" I ask him. With all we've experienced, he's earned such an honor.

He shrugs. "Go for it."

"Go for it?" I ask, frowning. I'm confused by his words of choice. "Does that mean yes?"

He grins, and it's one of my favorites, the one where he doesn't show any teeth. "Yes, that means yes."

I can't help noticing the tiny black fleck under the outside corner of his left eye and how his right eye is narrower than the left. There's a deep line that begins at the point of his chin and ends at his earlobe, and tiny specks of black hair dot his jaw and the skin above his top lip.

"Yes," I begin distractedly but quickly refocus on our conversation. "You can't ascribe belief to what is real. What is true is simply truth, not belief."

He studies me. I squirm because even though he's simply focusing on my face, there's still a burning desire in his eyes.

"I like you, Ad'ru. A lot," he confesses.

"You do?" I say in a strange, high-pitched voice. He's still making me nervous.

"Yeah." He's in front of me but reaching behind me.

I breathe deeply through my nostrils because his strong hands are kneading the rounds of my buttocks and pushing me into his firm organ.

"I want to kiss you," he says with his mouth close to mine.

I gulp. "You do?"

"But I don't want to be rushed." He kisses my cheek and steps back.

I'm baffled until Na'ta appears in the place where he once stood, just not as close.

"Here," she says, draping a pair of green pants and a black cotton, short-sleeved shirt over my shoulder. She drops a pair of black boots in front of me. "Put these on. And there are socks in there."

I notice she's wearing the exact same outfit.

She snaps her fingers. "Hop to it, Adore. We don't have much time to waste."

"You want me to hop?" I ask, confused.

"I meant hurry up and get dressed," she amends with patience and no mockery.

I glance at Chex and then Na'ta, both fully clothed. I've never felt more exposed. This is why I pick up the boots and scurry off behind a tree to get dressed.

"By the way, I'm Navi," Na'ta says to Chex as I take care to slip the pants on over the lower part of my body. "And you're Chex."

He snorts. "You say that like you've been enlightened?"

"I have. I know the legend. But not the face."

"And what do you know of my legend?"

"That you're a killer," she says. She sounds quite impressed.

He laughs loudly, and in my mind, I see him tilting his head back to bellow out that sound.

"Do I owe you apologies?" Chex asks as I slip on the second black boot.

I feel my face drop in disappointment when I

realize that I have to lace the boots. I've seen Na'ta tie her boots many times, but I've never had to do it for myself. Before Na'ta can respond, Chex is kneeling before me, lacing the string of one boot and then the other. I'm so enchanted by him that I run my fingers through his wavy black hair. But I quickly withdraw my hand, because I get a flash of truth.

"There," he says as he stands. "And, um, you didn't have to take your hand away." He holds out his arms and grins at me. "I'm yours for the taking."

I smile at him. He has no idea what alarmed me. When I touched the fibers on his head, I saw that the true color of his hair is not black but that of straw, like that of Baron Ze Feldis. His eye color is not truly black either. Why would a Selell go through so much trouble to conceal his identity?

"Shit, I forgot," Na'ta curses as she appears behind the tree. "Sorry about that, Adore. I keep forgetting you're no earthling."

"See." Chex affectionately taps my chin. "You're new." He winks at me.

I let the matter of his hair and eyes drop. I have often wondered how my sisters could trust so much in creatures who were conceived out of the ambitions of the evil. I always believed they are eternally tortured by their thirst and will manipulate and scheme to quench it. But now that I have close experience with Selells of my own, my beliefs are dissipating. Chex has not once threatened to harm me in any manner. Since we first fell in each other's company, he's only sought to protect me.

As we stare into each other's eyes, I can easily declare that he's my *tek ce'bek*, my friend. But not in the way that Tryst is my friend. I relish when Chex puts his hands on me, when he holds me close or asks permission to explore my *da'na'ra*, my body. I want to know everything about him. I want to have known him all of his life! I've been alive longer than he's been a human or Selell, I'm sure of it.

"Okay, enough of this," Na'ta hisses as she observes the staring between Chex and me. There's a warning in the way she's looking at me. "Tetra's calling."

"About that," Chex says, breaking eye contact with me. He rests his eyes on her.

For just a moment, I feel abandoned by him. What a strange emotion this is. However, I notice how those two words have instantly brought him Na'ta's full attention. I think it's the way he said it. She knows he objects to her plan.

"If you need Ad'ru's bond to get into Tetra, we can find him because I can smell him." Chex wrinkles his nose as if the scent of Exgesis is foul. "But you might want to ask Ad'ru if this is what she wants to do before you go leading her to some place where dead vampire souls go to rot."

"Not rot—to wait." Now she's frowning. "And her name is Adore. Don't speak Enuian if you're not Enuian, Selell."

Chex lifts his top lip to show his teeth, but this time, a guttural growl roars in his throat. "If *Ad'ru* has a problem with me calling her Ad'ru, then she'll tell me, not you."

"I don't have an issue with him calling me by my real name," I chime in.

"I do," Na'ta hisses. She looks just as sinister as Chex.

Like Chex, Na'ta has a sea of blood on her hands. She's not like me, or Cl'auta or Falu. She is more like Tapeetha. They both lust for the fight. Unlike Tapeetha, Na'ta spends her days seeking out battles. Once she walked right into a coven of hostile Selells with Telman. Naturally, a fight occurred. She was sliced across the face then pierced through the heart with a poisoned blade. Sometimes

I think none of us other than Na'ta could survive the wounds that befall her. Father healed her face then, but she has a long scar across her cheek which she received from the claw of a sea creature.

"Na'ta," I reprimand while taking her shoulders to force the light into her.

She rolls her angry eyes away from Chex and widens them at me. "I'm sorry, Adore. If you like him that much, then so be it. So you say you can smell him?" she asks Chex, controlling her anger.

It's safe to take my hands from her because the light has effectively subdued the part of her that is single-minded.

Chex snickers after witnessing how the power of light controls her. "I think I'm starting to believe in God," he mumbles. I realize he's being sarcastic. "So what now?"

"We find Adore's *true* bond," Na'ta says to upset him. The light couldn't stop her from taking that jab at him.

If Chex is bothered by what she said, he doesn't show it. He nods at me for my consent, and once again, the way he's looking at me takes my words away. I can only smile at him. He takes one deep, long inhale, closes his eyes, and carefully releases the tepid air. He smiles at me just like I'm still smiling at him.

"Got him," he says.

"I guess you have to lead the way," Na'ta says. She doesn't sound happy.

"Just remember your place is behind me," he jokes.

She snarls and rolls her eyes at him. He leaps off down a path, and we follow.

CHAPTER 7

BACK TO LIFE
ADORE

W̶e exit the forest, leaving the muddy daylight behind us. The change in environment is abrupt as we walk the wind in a night sky with billions of sparkling white *kets*, or stars. The same tall, sharp blades of grass that grow in the Mashlands coat the landscape beneath our feet, and a significant number of spiraling crop formations are strewn throughout. However, unlike the Mashlands, it's peaceful here. We're even being carried by a trail of cool, whispery breezes.

Chex storms ahead, leading us to Lario Exgesis. The tail of his black coat flows behind. I notice how comfortable he is keeping one hand hidden inside the coat. He hides weapons in the inseam, and I wonder if touching the instruments brings him solace. No words are spoken between us. Na'ta is using all of her concentration to attempt to connect with Telman. She hasn't stopped trying since we started over these strange lands.

My mind is drawing from lessons I have learned over time about the power of the i'lek'u. I recall my studies of the *lar'im,* the soul of a creature. Within it exists a light the size of a speck of sand. It's called the *a'hanterel,* and it's made of delicate tissue. Only I, Ad'ru, with the power of light, can access it. However, I have been entrusted to use the lar'im sparingly. My power enables me to know more about a being than it could even know about itself.

I have tried to connect to the energy that bonds me to Lario Exgesis, but he is quite learned in our ways. He has invoked a defense that can keep out even me. However, I am more knowledgeable than he can ever know. As we travel over a sea of sameness, Exgesis continues to saturate my thoughts. If he can keep me from connecting to him, then why isn't he able to obstruct Chex? He knows we are together. Even from his watery prison, he saw the Mtknv hand Chex to me as a companion. Now is the time to enter the a'hanterel of Lario Exgesis, and so that is what I do.

The i'lek'u knows who I seek, and once it latches onto him, my body comes to an abrupt stop. Even though my eyes are wide open, all I see is stark white light. I hear Chex and Na'ta asking if I'm okay, but it sounds as though they are far away.

At this very moment, I am contained in Lario Exgesis's lar'im. He's on muddy earth surrounded by huts of yellow straw and pink, fleshy, humanoid creatures with tiny black spikes growing out of their scalps. What peculiar beings they are, just as jarring as the Mtknv, the Mash, and the Guards of Siffeo. I instantly notice that these creatures naturally hold their mouths with the top lip curled over their blackened, decayed teeth. Their eyes are fully black, but there's a yellow dot in the center of them. Even as the creatures stand still and breathe, they sound like a wild pack of snorting Earth animals called wild boars. Lario knows them as the Treesh, and although he's repulsed by their anatomy, he takes care not to show it.

"Where's light and speed?" one of the Treesh creatures roars thunderously.

"Close," Lario Exgesis claims. He sounds sure of this, but deep down, he is not certain that his scheme will work. This is why he has draped himself in the light.

Gripped by anxiety, he looks at the sky. He's expecting us—me, Chex, and Na'ta. He conjured up his scent to have Chex guide us into the hands of these creatures, the Treesh, who reside in the bogs along the southern border of the territory that borders Ronoloh. He is playing two sides. He and the Olligark stole the Scepter of Gant from the Mtknv, who are its guardians. Now he's consorting with the Treesh to steal it from the Olligark. He's deceiving both factions. Exgesis is reliving every moment, and the images excite him.

"You get us the scepter or you die," the creature threatens.

Lario shrugs with smug nonchalance. He does not fear the Treesh creature's threat. If any of the Treesh creatures come in contact with the light, it will feel pain so severe that, although it won't die, it will want to die.

His a'hanterel has informed me well. He knows that Na'ta will seek to save Telman at any cost. Strangely, I am fervently in Exgesis's thoughts. He is vexed by the way I smell, even the tone of my voice, and how being near me rouses feelings that have never been alive in him before. Like a Selell craves blood, he craves me. However, more than he lusts for me, his bond, he is driven toward seeking ultimate power. I also see that Lario Exgesis doesn't want to yearn for me. That is why he is deliberately betraying me, in hopes that his aspirations will isolate us.

Then I understand why he covets the Scepter of Gant: it will make him king of all universes. I also see why Na'ta and I are needed to recover the instrument, and that's when it becomes clear to me that we must do what Exgesis wants and take the Scepter of Gant out of the Olligark's hands. We must return it to the Mtknv. It will never be safe in their hands as long as incessant invaders like the Olligark seek its power, but they are its rightful guardians.

I blink to focus once I'm fully back to myself. Na'ta grabs my shoulders and shakes me.

"You're back." She sighs in relief. "What the hell were you doing? We saw the light inside you; it was the only way we knew you weren't having a seizure or something."

I glance at Chex. He's scowling at me. I think I frightened him, and I am very sorry for that. After taking a few calming breaths to steady myself, I tell them what I just experienced.

"Then you stopped us just in time," Na'ta says, relieved. "This is Ronoloh. It's the empty land."

"The empty land?" Chex asks.

"Nothing lives here, and you can't stay here too long or the lohs will make fertilizer out of you." She narrows her eyes to study the ground. "The *loh* is the grass. *Ronoloh* means high grass. But we're safe; apparently the human in us doesn't taste like chicken."

Chex grunts, amused by her remark, but I don't understand. A chicken is an Earth creature, a fowl...

"Forget it, Adore," Na'ta says, noticing my puzzlement. "It was a joke."

"Oh." I look at the crop circle that swirls beneath us. I really feel "new" now, and I don't think I like it much.

"So why does he need your light and my speed?" she asks.

When I look up, I take a glance at Chex, who winks at me while wearing an endearing smile. My shame suddenly fades.

"He thinks we can use my light to get past the Olligark." I notice Chex crease his brows. I wonder what he's thinking, but I continue. "I believe they are in a universe called Ol."

"Yes, it is Ol," Na'ta confirms.

"So... like Exgesis, you're familiar with this

shit?" Chex asks Na'ta, but even I can detect the indictment in his tone.

"Screw you, vamp," Na'ta barks. "If you're trying to pin me to that psycho-maniac, then I'll kick your ass right here, right now!"

Chex rolls his eyes, clearly not intimidated, and snorts forcefully.

"Stop you two!" I scold. I'm weary of their bickering. "Answer the question," I demand of Na'ta.

She assesses the seriousness in my expression. I'm showing her a look she's familiar with. In all the years of my life, Na'ta is the only other creature who's moved me to anger.

"I know of them," she says bitingly, rolling her eyes from me to Chex then back to me. "Ol is a pitch-black universe. That explains why he needs your light." She pauses. "But why my speed?"

"Because you're able to carry me," I say as the revelation occurs to me.

"Ah," Na'ta breathes and looks off to reflect. "Humph. Why didn't I ever think of that?"

"What are you confessing, Na'ta? Have you antagonized these creatures before?"

She shrugs. "If I answer, you're going to give me that deadpan look of yours. That's why I choose to plead the fifth."

"What?" I shout. "What does that mean?" I'm nearly weary of her antics.

"She's saying yes," Chex answers as Na'ta stares at me with wide and worried eyes.

"One day, Na'ta." I shake my head, and my eyes water a little. "You will be the first of us to die from a murderous hand."

She tilts her head. "You should try frightening me with the possible."

We glare at each other. I know what she's referring to. Like Tapeetha, she doesn't fear death because she's tested the limits of our destructibility. They are both convinced we can't die.

"Whatever, Adore," she finally says with a shrug. "And apparently you're in charge here. So just promise me that we won't leave the alternate universes without going into Tetra." She lifts her eyebrows.

"I promise," I say sincerely.

She shifts her eyes away from me to Chex. "And you?" She waits for his answer.

I'm surprised she even asked. This is a civil act, and I'm proud of her.

"If she's in, I'm in," he replies with his gaze fixed on me. Then he scowls at her. "So where's this place—Ol?"

"Follow me." Na'ta darts downward to enter a corridor that's cut into the crop circle beneath us.

Tall blades of coarse grass dwarf us. The first thing I notice is that it's warmer down here than it was up there. It's never like that in Enu. The temperature stays the same whether in a cave, in a valley, on a mountaintop, or under the seas.

"And don't touch the grass," Na'ta warns.

"Duly noted." Chex slips off his jacket and spreads it on the ground. Just as I thought, he's carrying daggers and other sharp instruments. He has hundreds of them lined up and kept in place by loops from one hem to the other.

"The infamous arsenal," Na'ta says, studying each instrument carefully.

He lifts one side of his mouth into that lopsided grin, showing teeth. "You've heard."

"But none of that will work against the Olli-gark. I'll be back." Without another word, Na'ta invokes the power of speed, and she's gone.

Chex and I are once again alone. The lingering silence is awkward.

"I must say…" He rises out of his squat. He hesitates once I make eye contact with him. "I like how you handle your sister. She comes off all badass, but you're the real badass." He's leering at me.

I wonder what desires are veiled by the look in his eyes, but I am more curious about the meaning behind his words. "What is 'badass'?"

Still gazing at me in that manner, he moves forward until he's quite close. "A badass is someone with real control. You control me. You control her. Hell, you even control Ktkl!"

I smile. "You said his name." I'm happy he didn't call such a remarkable creation like Ktkl and his species "water people."

"You like that?" he asks in what I've noted is his seductive tone.

Rendered speechless, I'm only able to nod.

"I like you," he whispers.

My head feels as if it's floating away from my body, and I gulp the air that's trapped in my throat just to remind myself that I'm still in control of that part of my body. "I like you too," I croak in a squeaky voice.

We stare into each other's eyes. I wonder what he'll do next. Is he going to ask to touch me? Maybe kiss me?

Instead he says, "I still hate that you're bonded to Exgesis. I hate it a lot."

I touch his chest where his heart used to beat, without his consent. "I don't choose these things. If I could, I would choose you and not him."

"Shit." He sighs, and instantly his lips are on mine and his cold tongue is in my mouth.

This action between us... it's like a slow and steady search. The longer we exercise, the warmer our mouths become. My heart, my head, and every cell of my body beg him to merge into me. He lifts me off my feet, pulling me tight into his hollow chest and long, firm sexual extremity.

Suddenly he stops and presses his forehead against my mine. "I don't know what I'm going to do with you, Ad'ru." He exhales and takes a deep inhale. He's drinking in my fragrance.

His eyes are closed, and he faces the sky to fight a growl. I watch him closely. I'm no longer frightened by the way his fangs touch his supple bottom lip. Oh, how he just kissed me! I'm all flesh and blood and breath; he stirs the human in me. We stand still, waiting for these impulses to pass.

When he's recovered, he opens his eyes and gazes deep into mine. "No one's ever gotten to me like this. *Ever.*"

"Me neither."

"No." He shakes his head. "You don't understand. You've been in Fairytale Land. I've been a goddamned vampire. I don't fuck and drink the thirst away; I kill it away."

"I'm confused," I say, frowning. "I don't understand how you're using the word 'fuck.' You sometimes use it as a verb, other times you use it as an expletive, and also an adjective. Na'ta only uses it as an expletive and sometimes an adjective."

He throws his head back and releases a hefty laugh—I love the sound. It enlarges my smile. But then I'm on my back, on the prickly soil, and he's on top of me. Our lips are connecting, and our tongues dancing again. This time, his hand is under my shirt, and he's indulgently kneading my breasts. A moan crawls up my throat and escapes past my lips. Our tongues are no longer touching because he is sliding his around my firm, tingling nipple. What he's doing is very sensual. The sharp tickling in my thighs, my private parts, and my breasts has returned.

He takes my hand and guides it to his groin. "You feel this?"

It's hard, like a rod. "I do," I whimper; my words are slippery.

"I put this…" His hand is now inside my pants, and it touches me in a very hot and wet place. "In here." He slips a finger inside me, and out of me, inside and out, circles it and repeats the action.

I'm being devoured by pleasure. I'm panting. I can't think. What is this? I expand my eyes and try to look down to see what he's doing, but this intensity is wakening deep inside me. I hear a high-pitched cry, and I can hardly believe that I am the originator of such a shriek. I don't grow silent until that sensation subsides.

"Hey," Na'ta grunts.

I flick my eyes open. She's standing over us. Chex helps me quickly to my feet, and I stand with wobbly legs. He has an arm wrapped around my waist to steady me.

"I can't leave you alone with her for five minutes, can I?" she says, directing her anger at him.

"She's defiling me. It's not the other way around," he says.

"Whatever." She throws a black canvas bag at the arm he's using to embrace me.

He lets go of me to catch it before it hits me, which was her intention.

"See... She can stand on her *own* two feet," Na'ta says snidely.

Chex grunts dismissively and then focuses on

the bag as he pulls the drawstring. It unfolds, revealing an arsenal of peculiar objects attached to the material. Chex runs a finger down the edges of the sharp ones, slicing open his flesh. I expect blood to pour out of the wound, but it heals before that can happen.

"What the hell are these?" he wonders. He's sliding a finger down metal balls.

"Those are trikes," Na'ta says. "The Olligark are all bone. No skin. No flesh. They're like pure steel. Your blades won't be able to penetrate them, but all of that will."

"So we throw balls at them, and then what?"

"Correction"—Na'ta lifts her eyebrows as she drops the same kind of canvas bag off her back and onto the grass—"it takes at least five balls. Then *pow!*—they explode."

Chex grunts flippantly. "I won't need these."

"Oh yes, you will," she insists.

"And what about these?" he continues, ignoring her. He's touching objects shaped like various leaves.

Na'ta grins. "Those are gutters." Apparently she has a certain amount of affection for the weapons. "You'll never beat the Olligark in hand-to-hand combat, but these"—her grin deepens—"they can."

He frowns studiously at them. "How?"

"How good is your aim?"

"Flawless."

"Good. When the time comes, just let one go and watch it work," she sings.

They're sort of getting along, which I very much prefer to the squabbling. I try to push my memories of what I just experienced out of my mind as I watch them load up with these objects. He made me "come," as he called it. What a potent sensation.

I observe his hands as he swiftly puts the extra instruments inside his coat. There's preciseness in the way they move. He refuses to part with his Earth weapons, even after Na'ta offers to carry them to her compound in the kark forest. I sense he also has a strong emotional connection to them.

Na'ta dismantles the canvas bags and wraps parts of them around her waist and the upper part of each of her arms. She insists that I carry at least five trikes in each of my pockets, as well as a strip of gutters around my arm. Initially, I protest. My weapon is the light and only the light. But Na'ta suggests I hold these things "just in case." If I don't need them, then that's fine; but if I do need them, then I will have them. Chex strongly agrees. It is such a relief to see them in agreement that I decide to lug the weapons.

We ride the wind, but this time, we're journeying eastward.

"It's pitch black in Ol," Na'ta warns. "Wherever the Olligark go, they bring the darkness with them. I imagine that's how they were able to steal the Scepter of Gant. But we're going to travel through the southern end of Zrr. Their darkness doesn't work so quickly there." She stares farther into the distance. "They won't be able to get a jump on us there, even if they do see us coming. I'll outrace them, and Adore, you'll blind them with the light." Her tone is jovial, excited. For thousands of human years, this is how she's chosen to live her life—picking fights with strange beings.

"Are there creatures in Zrr?" I glance at Chex, and he's staring at me.

"Once upon a time, the Aarap lived there, but from what I know, the Olligark wiped them out."

"Is that so?" I ask, fascinated by the thought of another peculiar species. "What did they look like?"

"Lizards."

"So where the hell is this Scepter of Gant?" Chex asks. It's strange because I'm sure he's speaking to Na'ta, but he's still gazing at me.

"Are you asking me or her?" Na'ta asks snobbishly.

"You." He's short with her.

She sighs hard and rolls her eyes. "The hell if I know. But it can be in one of three places."

"I know where it is," I say before they can quarrel. "It's in an enormous spider made of stone."

The look on Na'ta's face asks me how I knew that.

"Exgesis's lar'im revealed it to me."

Chex shifts his eyes from me to stare straight ahead after hearing that name.

"Oh." Na'ta nods. "But no—it's not made of stone. It's made of bones. Those bastards kill one another to build their cities." She looks disgusted. "But that place you're referring to is called the Tarantula."

"Tarantula. The spider?" Chex asks without turning his head.

"Yeah." She chuckles cynically. "Trips me out too."

"You really know a lot about these worlds," I say, impressed by her scope of knowledge.

"That's because I get out, and you don't. Just think, Ad'ru, you're the first. You've had thousands of years to find all this shit out."

Chex gives me a curious side-eye glance. "Thousands of years? How old are you?"

"Eight thousand years old, give or take. But really, who's counting," Na'ta answers before I can.

"Get the hell out of here!" Chex is studying me, but in a different way. He's searching for something.

"The truth is," I say, shrinking under the intensity of his gaze, "I don't have an age. I was born, and now I live, and I'll live until I die."

"You won't die," Na'ta mutters.

"You're a fool, Na'ta, if you don't think we're susceptible to death."

Chex's eyes move back and forth between us.

"Then I guess I'm a fool." She winks at me with a smirk.

I shake my head. I'll never get through to her.

"What about you?" Chex asks Na'ta. "How old are you?"

"Older than you," she snaps, reveling in the fact that he asked. "Fifteen hundred, give or take." She only answered because she loves the way it sounds. The longer she lives, the more invincible she feels.

Chex doesn't say a word. He looks as if he's pondering something, as if he finally understands that we are not humans—we are truly unique beings.

All of a sudden, the environment changes. It's white and hazy all around us, but beneath us, the ground looks as if it's made of salt crystal. Bulky clusters of the material are spread across the terrain as far as my eyes can see. There's no tree or plant or flower or greenery of any kind in this universe. It's white and dreary and lifeless.

"Look," I say, pointing at the top of one of the clusters.

"I see it," Chex says, glowering at the strange creature.

"It's an Aarap!" Na'ta cries.

She was right. It looks like a lizard. Its very presence beckons us to stop in our tracks to study it. The creature has the body of a gigantic chameleon with scaly gray skin, a hunched back, and coiled tail. The heels of its two reptilian hind legs resemble a human's, but its toes are curved and clawed. The same goes for its arms, which are reptile-like with human palms and clawed fingers. Then there's the head: a cross between a tortoise and a man, with big white eyes that blink rapidly, purple lips, and two holes right in the middle of its face.

"I guess they're not all wiped out," Na'ta whispers, still marveling at the sight of the creature.

"Are they aggressive?" Chex already has one hand in his coat.

"No," Na'ta whispers, taking care to keep the volume of her voice low. "Not if we stay high."

The Aarap curves its neck so far that the top of its scabby head touches its bulging spine and lets out an ear-piercing hiss. It's so loud that I have to cover my ears with my hands. Loud rumbling mixes with the creature's hiss. The ground shakes, and although we are in the air, the quake rattles us too. I feel Chex's hard body against my back. He's holding me tightly. Then all at once, a vast number of Aarap creatures emerge from the depths of the salt crystal, their bulbous eyes fixed upon us.

The last thing I hear is Na'ta shouting above the noise, "Let's get out of here!"

But I'm covered in some sort of web that has me so bound, I can't struggle against it. Chex's arms are no longer around me, and I feel his absence. I try to gather my bearings as I'm pulled downward. Just when I think I should hit the surface, I don't. I'm unable to hear, see, or smell anything. I call the power of the light and force it out of every pore of my body. I'm waiting for the light to devour this weapon of evil and free me from this wicked web that has me bound.

Ad'ru, stay calm, Na'ta says to me telepathically.

I can't free myself... I try to squirm, but the web has me securely fastened.

I've stopped descending, and I'm lying on a hard surface. The fibers binding me begin to unwind until my mouth is freed and then my eyes. I can see again. When the rest of me has been liberated, I leap to my feet and press my back against Na'ta's as we instinctively take a defensive stance. Scores of reptilian creatures encircle us, but they are split between watching us and focusing on an enormous wall made of crystal where we can see two battles playing out on the surface of Zrr.

First, the Olligark have brought their opaque darkness. It tries to shove the hazy daytime out of existence, but the light refuses to concede. Using their stealthy arms, the Treesh are winding up a thick-linked chain with a solid stone ball attached to the end of it to deliver blows to the seemingly indestructible Olligark. If it weren't for their methods, the solid pink, human-like Treesh would be easily annihilated. They work in unison to bring the Olligark to their knees before delivering deathblows to their heads. Yet the Olligark are clearly winning. They fight with their skeletal hands, and once they clamp down on an opponent, they can rip their limbs apart, even those of the durable Treesh. Bubbling, thick purple blood and mammoth-sized bones coat the battlefield. I turn my face because the sight is difficult to absorb.

"The Ol," an Aarap says, rolling the *l* in Ol, "saw you through the eye of the world." The creature buzzes. It's not exactly speaking Enuian or English, but its words slither off its tongue in sharp hisses. "We honor our pact with that of Benel. We protect you in Zrr."

Na'ta cringes at the mention of our father's protection. "The eye? The Zkr?" Her voice rings with curiosity. "That means they lifted that from the Mtknv too."

"Wait," I nearly shout, realizing we're short one companion. "Where is Chex?" I twist and turn, searching frantically for him. My pulse races. I'm forced to gaze upon the violence and the slaughtering that has not ceased. I desperately search for him in the mess of bones, blood, and death.

"He is vampire..." the Aarap says in his decipherable hiss.

I'm hanging on his every buzz, wondering where his explanation will lead, when the Aarap's scaly head flies clean off its neck. It hits one of the crystal columns before dropping to the floor. All of the Aarap cry out in an uproar that's so deafening, it feels as if my head has split into two. To my left, I see Chex standing over the headless creature, grasping a dagger in each hand. He fixes his eyes on the nearest Aarap and is on the verge of calling his reflexes in motion. He's quick, but for the grace of the Creator, I'm faster. I get in front of him and grab his massive shoulder.

His eyes are glazed over as he curls his neck to observe my grip on him. Before I can shout his name over the incessant buzzing, he shoves me away. I fly through the air until Na'ta catches me, stopping me from hitting a column. At the same time, I see blurs of Chex as he evades the Aaraps' streaming web.

The Aaraps grow angrier, judging by the intolerable noise they're making. But Chex is also mad. It is clear they will duel to the death. Without hesitation, I pull the light out of me and fill the entire space with it. The daggers drop out of Chex's hands and clink against the durable crystal. The Aaraps stop shooting their constraining string.

"What the hell just happened?" Na'ta mutters.

She's watching me closely; they all are. I walk over to the head Aarap. Its eyelids are still blinking, and no blood of any sort oozes out of the cleanly sliced wound. I bend over to pick up the head and take it to its body, which is crumpled on the floor. Unlike the head, the body is not alive.

I know what I must do. I fit the head back in place on the creature's neck. That's when its eyes close, and it's finally at rest. I rub my hands over its skin. The texture is rough but warm. The Aarap is consumed with goodness. There's no evil within this species, which makes it easier for the light to work. After a moment, the body and head both glow; the Aarap reclaims life and flips over to stand on all four legs. The creature shows its gratitude by opening its mouth and licking me on the forehead. It tickles. I smile tentatively at the Aarap because nothing has changed; we are still in the same sticky predicament.

"I apologize for the Selell," I say. "He is a creature of war."

"He is of *ek*," the Aarap buzzes, *the evil* in my native language. "He cannot rest here in our universe."

I look at Chex, standing there, still dominated by the light. My gaze caresses him sympathetically. He is loyal, and he cares. He has helped me get this far, striving toward *my* objectives, not his own. Those are not traits of *dek ek*, the evil. The evil is self-centered and aids none beyond its own ambitions. It cannot conjure affection for any being outside of itself.

"I understand," I'm forced to say, because those are the laws of this universe. "But he is traveling with us, and he must go where we go. If he's banished, then we all must be banished with him." I widen my eyes at Na'ta, which is my way of asking for her support.

She sighs hard, shows me a tiny roll of the eyes, and nods once. "Any ideas on how to cross over into Ol without being seen by the Eye of Zkr?"

Without moving its head, the Aarap shifts his eyes nervously toward Chex.

"He's subdued," I promise.

The creature slithers toward Chex and circles him. The Selell does not move. He remains under the control of the light, although he eyes the creature cautiously.

"The *darampeer* cannot escape the eye within our borders. It is why you were discovered," the Aarap squeals.

"*Darampeer* is the Selell?" I clarify.

"Yes," the Aarap hisses, still circling Chex. "With the i'lek'u of Benel, he may enter Ol of the

Olligark, but only through the portal of the Ugu Mag of Dag, the plane of the separated humans."

Chex wiggles his shoulders and stretches his neck from one side to the other, slowly coming to himself. I'm relieved. He's regaining mobility because he's choosing to partner with the light and not fight its control. The Aarap who's slithering around him moves away and unleashes a loud shrill. It is an alarm of safety, letting the others know that Chex has accepted the light and they are safer.

"*Ugu Mag*?" Na'ta frowns thoughtfully. "The first people? Never heard of them."

"They have been separated," a second Aarap says. "They are of soil of the earth, warm blood, and the wind of Elrrzz."

"Wait…" Chex manages to speak while shaking his head. "Humans? You're asking us to trust humans? Listen, if there's a scepter up for grabs, you better believe those bastards have their eyes on it already."

I have no option but to nod in agreement, and so does Na'ta. Our chances of capturing the Scepter of Gant are greatly diminished if we're putting our faith in the hands of mankind.

"Are they men and women of vanity and war?"

I ask, although I presume to already know the answer.

"How can they be?" the Aarap sizzles in shock. "The lips of evil do not whisper in Dag or walk its wind."

We look among ourselves, gauging each other's reactions. What would that be like, encountering a species of humans uninfluenced by *dek'ek*?

"Will you show us the way?" I ask, completely enthralled by the idea of facing the Ugu Mag of Dag.

The large crystal panel that displayed the battle between the Olligark and Treesh is completely black. I realize that the Olligark have prevailed, and the surface of Zrr is pitch black. It's a daunting sight, but right before our eyes, the view disintegrates into swirling light-blue clouds.

"Enter," the Aarap hisses.

We all gaze at what will be our next destination.

CHAPTER 8
DAG LUST
ADORE

Night has fallen here in Dag. A bright full moon hangs in the southeastern sky, and its rays trickle smoothly across our faces. We are standing on one of many black tar roads that crisscross and hang in midair.

"How is this even possible?" Chex mutters to himself.

"But there's gravity here," Na'ta says, looking at her feet. "I don't understand how they were able to do this. This universe is a carbon copy of Earth, right?"

She's asking me, but I have no answer. I'd never heard of the Ugu Mag of Dag until the Aarap creature told us about it.

"It was simple," a voice says from behind us.

We all whip around to face a fully human female.

"Gravity is energy, and the Makers are able to transform the consistency of its force to build up high. Do you approve?" she asks, smiling warmly.

"Is it for us to approve?" I ask, as Na'ta and Chex scowl at her. It's interesting how alike my sister and the Selell are.

"Yes, it is," the woman gently says.

"Then we approve," I answer for us all.

The woman studies my face and then Na'ta's. I can't help but observe her as well. She's wearing a garment that's like the pal'k, but instead of white, it's brown like the bark of a tree. It suits her sand-colored skin, crimped black tresses, and discerning gray eyes.

"Navi and Adore," she says at the end of her examination.

Na'ta and I exchange stunned looks.

"How do you know us by sight? I've never seen you," Na'ta' says as she dips her chin and squints one eye.

"Because you are the daughters of Benel."

"That I know. But who the hell are you?" she says so impolitely I cringe.

I often wish she would be less abrasive.

"I'm the Transporter of the Gateways in and out of Ugu Mag," the woman answers, unaffected by Na'ta's tone. "My name is Jumangu Luganum; that translates to Magnificent Star."

Na'ta blatantly rolls her eyes in response, but our host doesn't appear to notice. Instead she glances at Chex. She sees what I see. He's slightly wobbly on his feet, and his face is damp.

Feeling the weight of losing time, I tell her all about the Mtknv and the Scepter of Gant and how we must take it from the Olligark and return it to the Mtknv.

"It can't be returned to them," Magnificent Star says, resolutely shaking her head. "They're too vulnerable, and the Olligark will just take it back."

"Yes, I know," I concur. "But it's rightfully theirs."

"Then you already knew it was stolen?" Chex asks, raising an eyebrow suspiciously. "What, you think it'll be safer here?"

Magnificent Star shoots a quick look at Na'ta, one I almost miss, before saying, "Emblems and trinkets of evil cannot remain in Dag."

"You're telling me you don't have any designs on such a powerful *trinket*?" Chex asks dubiously.

"No. We don't deny that the very essence of humanity is to seek certain power. We have our struggles, just like the humans on Earth, but we have an advantage. Evil is not allowed into our realm; therefore we don't seek to dominate. Our goal is only to expand our minds, hearts, and universe."

"Ha!" Chex scoffs. "I don't buy it. If you're trying to convince us that if it weren't for this mean, evil force, humans wouldn't be violent, power-hungry shitheads, then your efforts are lost on me."

Magnificent Star takes two strong steps to Chex. "You forgot envious, rapacious, and domineering. Yes, we have the ability to manifest those traits, but we do not. And anyway, my goal is not to convince you. I'm here to help you."

"Why?" He grunts. His skin is wet and clammy.

"Because the Daughters of Felix Benel are here. That is why."

"Because they showed up?" His tone is colored by sarcasm.

"Yes."

"Wait. Then how did he get in?" Na'ta motions toward Chex. "He's a vampire."

"Do you crave blood?" Magnificent Star asks him.

He sighs and shakes his head.

"Then he is cleared to enter Dag." She studies him for a few moments. "We should move forward; we have a lot to do." She walks to the edge of the road where there's nothing in front of her but air. "And do not be concerned when I jump. The degrees of gravity will guide me safely to the landing pod." She faces forward and steps over the edge.

"What the hell?" Na'ta exclaims as she hurries to search over the edge. "Oh." She sounds relieved. "There she is." She looks over her shoulder to glance at me. "We're next; let's go." She steps over the edge as well.

She's expecting me to follow without hesitation, but when I turn to Chex to make sure he's ready to walk over the edge with me, he takes my arm and pulls me into him.

"I'm sorry for throwing you back there," he says.

I hardly remembered him tossing me out of the way so that he could attack an Aarap creature. "You were filled with rage and revenge. It wasn't personal."

"No," he mumbles. "No excuse…"

All of a sudden, I'm lifted off the road into his

embrace. I'm keenly aware that his tongue is not cold but warm in my mouth. His body is warm too. I feel his heart beating against my chest.

"Chex," I manage to puff through our heavy kissing. I want to ask if he's alive, but my mouth can't stop receiving his. My head feels as if it's twirling on my shoulders.

"I'm dying for you, Ad'ru," he whispers.

I want to fall deeper into ecstasy with him, but Na'ta is yelling at me to hurry up and join them.

"Chex," I breathe as he runs his tongue around my lower lip before indulgently consuming it. "You're more human here…"

He stops kissing me and presses his forehead against mine. "I know. That's why I can't restrain myself any longer. I love you. Shit, I love you." His eyes are shut tightly as he says this.

I press my hands to his cheeks, concerned because his skin has grown warmer. Not even warm but hot—smoldering hot. He's even more unsteady on his feet. I wrap my arms tightly around his strong waist and try to steady him.

"Let's see if we can get you some rest," I say and guide him over the edge of the road.

We're dropping fast although we're in full

control of our speed. Chex is shivering. He seems to be struggling to keep his eyes fully open, and sweat pours out of him. Oh goodness, he is ill. I'm anxious, wondering if we'll ever hit bottom. We pass layers upon layers of these roads, and I find myself cursing their existence.

What's taking you so long? Na'ta is back inside my head.

It's Chex. Something's wrong with him.

His head flops down on the top of mine.

What's wrong with him, other than the obvious?

He's become ill, I say, although I'm not sure what she means by "the obvious."

He can't be ill. We need him to get into Tetra! she whines.

Then I see it, a sprawling—and yes, floating for sure—city with thousands of buildings made of aluminum or steel or a similar material. Some of them have glass windows, but most have slots opened to the bright light of the moon. Some are shaped like circles or squares or rectangles or other odd shapes. Even while frantic, I take in as much of this new world as I possibly can because it surely is a sight to behold.

Our feet touch down in the center of a round

sponge, which hovers above a bright-green turf that is by no means grass, although it appears to be. I struggle to support Chex's weight because he's become quite heavy. Na'ta races over to tuck herself under his other armpit.

"What happened to him? Why is he like this?" she asks apathetically while scowling.

"I don't know." I feel the urge to lecture her about her lack of empathy, but now is clearly not the time. I cut my eyes away from her to focus fully on Magnificent Star. "We have to get him some help."

"We have cure pods but…"

"No!" Chex cuts her off, mustering up enough energy to vehemently object. "Just rest."

He sounds so weak that I can hardly stand it. I'd rather take him to the cure pods. The Ugu Mag are a sector of humanity who have figured out how to change the consistency of gravity to erect cities in the sky. Surely they can cure whatever ails him.

"I'll take you to the dorm of Felix Benel," Magnificent Star says. "Where the vampire can fully recover."

"Shit, why now…" Na'ta grumbles.

Together we're able to easily lift Chex and

follow Magnificent Star up a concrete-like path that appears after she touches a yellow glass strip hanging in midair.

"Hey…" Chex whispers groggily in my ear as we race up the path. "I can trust you?"

"Always…"

Only then is he secure enough to completely give in to sleep.

"He's not your bond," Na'ta mutters her warning.

I don't reply. If her attempt is to anger me, then she has succeeded. I feel something deeply for Chex. He's proven to be valiant and even patient. I would venture to say he's good-natured too. Therefore, at the moment, all I allow myself to think about is how the hike up the walkway feels as though it's taking forever. Finally we step off the path and are carried about two feet through the sky and into one of the windowless cavities. It's an empty room with gray marble-swirled walls.

"Remain still," Magnificent Star says, standing beside a yellow glass panel attached to the wall. It lights up as soon as she touches it, and once it's activated, objects that appear to be furniture become visible across the floor. "Most of the flat is furnished, using energy binding instead of textiles. It keeps our environment free of toxins."

I notice a yellow sofa, two matching armchairs with end tables beside them, and an oblong glass table with a diamond centerpiece that sprouts little tiny sickles of glass that curve like branches of kark trees.

"Where do we lay him down?" Na'ta asks, looking around. She sees that I'm struggling. Her strength is greater than mine since her power is derived from the physical and mine from the mental.

Magnificent Star walks behind the couch, leading us toward a cozy hallway. "This way."

"Let go of him. I'll carry him from here," Na'ta orders.

I hesitate but do as I'm told. She's like a streak of light that races into the corridor. It only takes an iota of time before it seems as if she's disappeared. Her power of speed is fascinating. I remember when she was a child and first discovered she possessed the power. She was definitely a "handful," as Father called her, making it difficult for us to keep up with her.

My limbs feel as light as a whispery wind since I am no longer sharing the burden of carrying Chex, although I miss his nearness. The corridor is short, and I stop in front of Magnificent Star, who is standing right outside the opening to a room that has a door made of cloudy light. Unable to fully express my gratitude, I stare into her eyes.

"He will recover shortly," she says.

Something tells me she knows exactly what's ailing him, but I am too anxious to ask, and I lack the patience to listen to an explanation. Instead, I take her hand and squeeze it, injecting her with the light of gratitude. She closes her eyes to drink it in as it fills her with the warmth of good.

"Thank you," she whispers.

"You're welcome."

We share a smile before I walk through the door. Na'ta has already laid Chex on an actual bed, although he doesn't look too comfortable curled up on the white linens. His eyes are still closed. He's still shivering but only mildly.

"You should get him undressed, Ad'ru," she says, looking at him while standing at the foot of the bed. "And get him under the covers. I think his body is in shock from entering this new place." After a moment of observation, she says, "It looks like he's turning back into a human or something."

"Or something." I sigh, watching him. It's

strange because he's not so pale, and although his body is behaving as if it's ill, he looks serene.

"Really, Adore, what's going on between you two? Are you in love with him?"

"Yes," I reply with assuredness.

"Why? You just met him."

"I know we just met."

"I thought you loved Tryst?"

I glance at her. Her eyes are pinned on Chex.

"I do," I say. "Tryst is my friend. Chex is more than that to me. He's my…" I think of how to express what I'm feeling. "He's my body."

I am sure I hear a tiny bit of empathy in her tone. "Well, it had to happen one day. Just promise you won't forget that I'm your favorite person."

I turn to look at her. She's watching me with wide, hopeful eyes and a slight smile.

"Na'ta," I say as she rests her head on my shoulder.

"Am I being selfish? Tell me if I'm being selfish," she implores.

"Of course you are," I say with a tiny chuckle. "But I understand. You will always be a priority to me. As I am *your* priority."

"I doubt it," she mutters. "I have never been for you what you are to me."

"That's because I haven't tested you in the ways that you've tested me."

"That's true." She chuckles. "Oh, but you love it, Ad'ru."

"No, it's you that I love. I hate your insolence."

"Insolence?" she blurts. Her head flies off of my shoulder as she winces.

"Yes. Insolence."

Her sigh is long and dramatic. "No one does the sweet-and-sour thing better than you, Adore. Never lose that, please... Your insults? Ah..." She presses a hand dramatically on her heart.

She's being cynical, I know, so I don't respond. It's the best way to make her stop. We watch Chex as he shifts from lying on one side of his body to the other.

"He is a good-looking vamp, in the rugged sense of the word," she says then turns to look at the doorway. "I'm going to step out and leave you to him..."

"Wait," I take her by the arm before she can leave. "Where are you going?"

"Magnificent Star wants to show me something."

"What does she want to show you?"

"I don't know," she says with a shrug. "I'll let you know when I do."

As soon as I let go of her, she disappears, leaving me alone with Chex. I wonder what to do next. I have never nursed an ailing creature other than my sisters. I start by taking one of his feet, untying the dusty black boot, and tugging it off. I do the same to the other boot. He makes an abrupt move and flips on his back, groaning.

When he's still and settled into the mattress, I unbutton, unzip, and slide his dusty pants down his legs. I hadn't noticed the tiny hairs budding out of his epidermis until this very moment. It's very odd. Tryst doesn't grow hair on his body, only his head. My sisters and I are the same. Invoking the permission he gave me to touch him whenever I want, I rub his leg to get a full sense of the fibers, but it's the muscles that enchant me. What a strong being he is.

When I go to take off his coat, he springs to consciousness and wraps his long fingers around my wrists, squeezing them tightly. After a moment of looking me in the eyes, he lets go, and his hand flops back down on the mattress. I finish taking off his jacket. It's very heavy as I lay it on the stone floor beside the bed. Then I take his shirt by the hem and lift it over his head. He's completely naked.

I can't help but notice that his man part isn't firm. I stare at it, wondering when it will become erect. All of a sudden, he flips onto his side and wraps his arm around my hips, causing me to stumble. I lose my balance and plop down on the side of the bed in front of him. Once I'm seated, he slides closer.

"Lay with me," he says lethargically.

He has me so tight, and he's not going to let go. I bend over to unlace my boots, kick them off, and pull off my very uncomfortable pants. Chex is not so out of it that he loosens his grip on me. I slip out of Na'ta's shirt, and once I raise my legs to lie beside him, he pulls me into him, moaning as my backside becomes firmly fixed against his front. The rigidness has returned to his man part, and his full breaths hit warmly against the back of my neck. My entire body rises and falls with his panting.

"Ad'ru..." One of his hands rides down the round of my hips. He releases a sigh when his fingers slip into where I am warm and moist.

I flip onto my back as one finger slides in and out of me like before. Does he even know what he's doing to me? His eyes are still closed, yet his lips are parted, and to my complete shock, he has no fangs. His finger is indulgently circling my clitoris. The movement is constant and gentle; I sense how soft I am against his finger. My breaths are heavy, and I'm whimpering under his control.

"Shouldn't you rest?" I whisper while containing the sparks of pleasure that are on the verge of exploding inside me.

"I can't if you're this close," he says.

"Then I should leave."

"No." He draws me deeper into his virile body.

He's not shivering anymore, and I'm full of desire.

"I want to make love to you. Will you let me?" he begs.

"Make love to me?" I'm confused by that vernacular. How does one "make" love?

"Yes…" He's still only speaking in whispers. "That's what I want. I crave you like I craved blood."

"If that's what you want, then yes." I think I know what I'm agreeing to.

Before I know it, he has mounted me, my legs are spread wide, and his hips are between them. I feel pressure first as his hand guides his man part into my female cavity. A piercing gasp escapes me.

He freezes. He searches my face with his heavy brows crinkled with concern. "Did I hurt you?"

I shake my head after pausing to assess what I feel. "No, I don't feel pain. What I feel is just—different."

"Do you like it?"

I nod against a pillow. "Very much." There's passion in my tone. I don't even recognize my own voice.

His hips shift back and forth. His movement is slow and deep as he sings a series of gasps and grunts.

"How does this feel?" he whispers.

How does it feel? I feel as if my heart will explode because it's so full of love for this Selell. Is that what making love means? He's inside me, and I want us to stay like this until time never ends. I lift my mouth to his, and he takes over, kissing me deeply. His firm man part slides in and out of me. Deeper. Faster. The speed with which he moves makes me tingle inside. Then he slows his pace and moves methodically.

"How about right here?" He's looking me in the

eyes as he directs his man part to his right, my left. "You didn't tell me how it feels."

I'm unable to tell him. Whatever this sensation is, it's keeping me from speaking. The only sounds I can make are moans and breaths. I shut my eyes tightly. My entire face and body are tense. Oh my! It's happening. The more he does that, the closer it comes—the *coming* is coming.

"Tell me, Ad'ru," he demands.

I open my mouth and cry out. This sensation is powerful and lasting. Chex wraps his arms around me and squeezes me into him as he grunts. He's experiencing pleasure too. We are undergoing it together. When our song ends, Chex isn't finished. My hard nipple is in his mouth, and he's still firm inside me, moving back and forth.

"You're soft, brand new," he whispers as he takes my other nipple between his lips and gently grazes it with his teeth.

I immediately feel the sensation. I want to ask him whether he even realizes that he's no longer a Selell. He's a man. Na'ta was right; this universe has changed him.

"You're brown and sweet, like maple." His tongue slides down my sternum, past my belly, and onto my clitoris, where he latches on.

I believe it's his tongue that's circling it, over and over, making me squirm. The sensation is overpowering. I clutch the sheets and then his shoulders. He grabs my hips to keep them still, refusing to relent. After I let out a cry, he doesn't stop. I whisper his name, and he doesn't stop. I moan, grunt, and sing out again, and still, he doesn't stop.

"Chex, please," I cry, begging as my female dome absorbs the explosion.

Before the sensation ends, he puts himself inside me again—thrusting and groaning. He knows exactly what he's doing to me, playing my body like a harp. He is the musician, and the notes are precise.

"I don't want to stop," he says as he rests heavily on top of me. "I don't want you to ever do this with Lario Exgesis. Will you promise me that?"

"I promise." There's no way I will ever engage in such an intimate act with any being other than Chex. I have made my vow, and it is so.

He stops to gaze at my face. I automatically memorize the curves around his mouth, the supple pink in his lips, and his straight nose, strong jaw lines, and high forehead. What a remarkable creature he is. Is this what a man looks like? Are such features his allure? They're so different from mine.

His are powerful, indestructible. Mine are feminine and tender.

"Shit, I believe you." He sighs after completing his study of me. "I've never believed anybody in my life, and I believe you, Ad'ru."

We kiss again. I love kissing him. We roll around on top of the bed. Our legs weave around each other. My fingers are on his back, in his hair, grasping his waist, his shoulders. The skin of our faces mesh. I am energized by the desperate sounds we make.

He pants as he shifts a portion of my hair that has fallen between our mouths out of the way. "You have long hair. You all do."

"Yes," I say between more kisses.

"It's sexy."

"It makes you want me?" I wonder.

"No… *You* make me want you." His lips and tongue smash deeper into mine. "Shit. I can't stop."

"You do know that you're human?" I whisper as he gnaws on my neck.

And now, he stops. One quick kiss and Chex goes to stand at the window. I admire his naked body as he gazes at the full, bright moon. His bare back faces me, and I can't help but admire the lines of his masculine physique. He is sullen. I keep my distance because it's clear that he finds venturing inside himself comforting.

Memories of him making love to me make me quiver. Even I must take stock of myself as I sit against the headboard with my arms wrapped around my legs. The side of my face rests on my knees. Watching him muddies my thoughts. He is a glorious creature. His bravery and loyalty first caused my affection for him. I turn my head in the opposite direction to stare at the room. I vaguely wonder where Magnificent Star has taken Na'ta. What could she possibly have to show her that couldn't wait until Chex recovered?

"Hey," Chex calls, and he comes over to turn my face back toward him. "What are you thinking?" He stares into my eyes, patiently expecting an answer.

"I'm confused," I whisper.

"About me?"

"I've never felt what I feel for you. If I'm bonded to Lario Exgesis, then I don't understand why I feel like I'm bonded to you."

He takes my hand and guides me to my feet. Once I'm standing, he wraps me in his arms and holds me close. I feel his man part rise against me.

"If you keep this up, I'm just going to live inside you," he says, chuckling.

"So it's because of me that you grow firm."

He tosses his head back to release a hearty laugh. I watch him with delight. I remember when I first laid eyes upon him. He was such a miserable creature, emanating evil. And the blood on his hands… Now when I look at him, I see that he is still that Selell, the one with his weapons and hands of death, but I know his heart.

"Does being human again trouble you?"

He takes a long, contemplative pause. "Something is happening to me, but I'm not human. Not all the way." He snarls. "I hate humans. I've known them for too many goddamn years. I don't feel like those monsters, and they are monsters, Ad'ru. They just are." He pauses, searching for objection in my expression.

I feel no need to object twice. I've already explained to him how I feel about referring to creatures as monsters, and he understood me perfectly well. Telling him once is enough.

"But I am starving," he continues. "I'm thirsty, not for blood but for water. Cold water. I'm starving for more of you. Hell, the craving I have for you makes me feel more like a vampire than the thirst for water makes me feel human."

"How did you use to quench your thirst for blood?" I ask out of sheer curiosity.

"I had mules."

I can tell he doesn't want to discuss it, but I do. "Mules?"

"Humans who fed me their blood. I'd pay them. And there were some I didn't have to pay."

"Why not?"

He hesitates. I can see him deliberating whether or not he should answer my question.

"They were women," he says. "They liked me."

"Oh." Goodness, I feel a pinch of jealousy. I picture him standing here naked with another female, and I despise the vision.

I step backward, and he moves forward, guiding me to the bed. Once the back of my thighs hit the edge of the mattress, he lifts me, cradling me in his arms.

"But none of them meant a damn thing to me. Remember when we were in the bar in New Orleans?" he asks.

"The bar in New Orleans?" I repeat. Of course, Bourbon Street!

He laughs. I can see what he's thinking. *I am new.*

"That was the first time I held you. You're the reason I came back. At first, I thought, 'What an ass.' Then I thought, 'She's damn soft.' Then I thought, 'There's no way Lario Exgesis gets her.'" Chex leans over, picks up a pillow, and puts it between us. "Here, lay down on top of this." He twirls me around to face the bed and gently guides me down on top of the pillow. His breathing has accelerated. His hands knead my rear. "Your ass is…unmatched. Are you aware of that?"

I reach back to feel my buttocks. "I'm not sure."

He chuckles. "You're so damn new." His whisper is tainted with lust.

He takes my hips, spreads my legs, and from behind, he guides his man part into my female cavity. I gasp, moaning to the pleasure of him crashing inside me.

"You're going to love this, baby," he says huskily, shifting in and out of me. "You see, the vampire feels you throbbing, pulsating. He feels your pussy showing him what it likes. We're communicating, baby."

I inhale a gasp and then unleash the second refrain of pleasure.

NAVI

This plane blows my mind. Human beings living like this! I had to escape Adore and Chex. There was no way I could stop him from deflowering her. Although I must admit he relishes her, like a bond would protect and revere his lifeblood. But what's crazy is that he's not her bond! So how in the hell was he able to slip through a portal? I'm sure he can smell his own blood. He would know if he were of Gogulon, wouldn't he?

MS, or Magnificent Star, has taken me pretty far away from where the two of them are getting it on. For a second, I wonder how it feels to screw a vamp who isn't a bond. Fawn is the only sister I know who has had experience outside the ultimate pleasure of screwing a bond, and she said it was good in a different way. According to her, it takes longer to have an orgasm, but once it arrives, it's still pretty spectacular. I asked her because I just wanted to know how it feels, not try it for myself. Sex is amazing, but my life gives me just as much pleasure.

For fourteen hundred of my fifteen hundred

years, I've been hunting relics. If Adore was asked, "What has Navi been doing for all of her life?" she would say something like, "Oh, Na'ta has been bumming around willy-nilly." She wouldn't use those words exactly—I live for the day when words like "bumming" and "willy-nilly" become part of her vocabulary.

My patience has worn thin, but I have to let Adore experience her first intimate encounter. As I've been trudging along with MS, my incessant search to see at least one other Ugu Mag has kept me entertained. But all I see are towers. This sea of banality is not good for a mind like mine. It gets me thinking about senseless shit like this.

"Hey," I say to MS, "do I have to call you Magnificent Star? It sounds kind of porn-starish."

"I know what a porn star is," she says without breaking stride. "And I prefer that you call me Magnificent Star. My given name was decided for me at birth. It's the very essence of who I am."

That was an expected reply, and one that I find quite amusing. She and Adore will get along perfectly.

"Not even Mag Star?" I persist. Only because, like my sister, I think she's being inanely inflexible.

It's just a name, and one that's five syllables too long.

She looks at me without turning her head. "You are contentious, Navi." She pauses thoughtfully. "Does it pain you to call me Magnificent Star?"

I shrug. "Kind of. Every time I say it, all I see is you wearing a long blond wig and blue eye shadow while humping a pole."

Then, unexpectedly, she laughs. Good God, she has a sense of humor! I take it back—she might not get along just fine with my humorless sister.

"A stripper's name?" she says with unmasked amusement.

"Yeah," I say as my laughter simmers. "How does the profession translate from Earth to Dag?"

She says quickly, but without judgment, "We have no such vocation on Dag."

I can't help but laugh. "Vocation? Now that's an upgrade!" I leave the door open for a comeback, but she smiles, tight lipped, deciding not to engage me in cynical banter. "So," I say as we continue to journey up the raised sidewalk that spirals around an oblong skyscraper, "how did you educate yourself on the wiles of Earth?"

"I'm a Transporter of the Gateways. My studies

make me knowledgeable about what is beyond our realm."

"So you see how calling you Magnificent Star tortures me? I don't want to picture you that way. You're too classy for that." I smile and wink at her.

She concedes with a sigh. "Call me what you prefer then."

I did it. I won. I feel myself grinning, satisfied as I gaze out at the dangling skyscrapers. I'm bored again now that that's over. We still haven't run into another soul, which is unheard of in a city of this size, even for one that floats. At night, all cities are crowded with horny humans looking to get hammered or screwed or both.

"Where the hell is everybody? Is there a curfew?" I ask.

"No, no curfew."

"Humph," I grunt, curious. "Well, are there any bars? Restaurants? Nightclubs?"

"The city is for enterprise, not for living," she coolly replies.

"But you said you weren't wasteful." There's a judgmental quality in my tone.

"Why would we live in the sky when we have the lands?"

We've finally made it to the top of this tower

that has to be at least five hundred feet high. We walk into it through an archway.

"Stay on the blue," Mag Star says.

A blue-lit strip splits the white stone floor. Right away, I fight the urge to veer off of the path, only because I'm naturally contrary. The space is open air, like a gymnasium. I can't help but wonder where the symbols of enterprise are. Where are the computers, the sleek receptionist, the sharp, modern couches that configure the waiting area? Where are the workers in their clinking heels or plunking loafers bustling about? I've infiltrated places like that before, and this seems more like a library or a museum, not a place where business exists.

Although I'm still itching to step off the blue, I decide to respect the boundaries, especially since I can see where we're headed. I squint curiously at what looks like an exposed elevator shaft straight ahead.

"Where are the lands? Is that where you're taking me?" I'm momentarily thrilled about the possibility of seeing where the Ugu Mag live and not work.

"I'm taking you to the hub."

"The hub?" I can't disguise my disappointment.

"The hub," she repeats.

We turn silent, but I'm bothered by hearing my boots clunk across the clean floor. I feel out of place. It's too spotless here for me. I never feel the need to conform, but right now, I kind of wish my boots were less grimy.

Anxiously, I glance at Mag Star. All of this is right up her alley. In her little brown dress and round-toed wooden shoes with S-shaped heels, she looks impeccable. I want to ask her to explain the shoes. With all the advancements in technology, why not a sleeker shoe? But I'm sure she has a good, practical reason for the wood and the shape of the heel. After all, this is the world of no strippers, nor drunk or horny humans.

Finally, we reach the exposed elevator shaft. I stretch my neck to look over the threshold. Before I can ask where the hell she's taking me, a female automaton voice warns me to "clear seam."

I immediately draw back to clear the doorway. A silver door slides down and then shoots back up. I flinch, surprised to see three men and one woman standing in a glass encasement. Seeing us, they scoot to one side to make room. Mag Star enters, but I become aware that I'm staring at their slight smiles and their dark-green clothes, which look like stiffly ironed hospital scrubs. After refocusing my thoughts, I take the space next to Mag Star that the Ugu Mag cleared for me.

There's a beep. "Clear seam for closing," the automaton warns.

The door slides close. I roll my eyes up to brace myself for what might happen next. I see the bright night sky above us. Smirking, I think the words for it are "majestic modernism." The glass cylinder drops.

"So I give: why the tour?" I finally ask her. "What's this all about?"

"What are you hiding?" she asks.

I quickly turn to search her face. That look. Does she know?

I gulp.

ADORE

"Isn't the moon very close?" I whisper in the cool darkness.

I'm not only in love with Chex, but I have come to love the night. Like him, it's intimate. It's alluring. I exhale as we stand naked on the threshold of the opened window. This city is uniquely wonderful. He's behind me, and his hands are flat on my belly. I feel as though I belong to him and we are in a place more perfect than home.

His lips graze the side of my face and then kiss my skin. "I think we should stay here. What about you?"

I gently sigh at the thought of residing in Ugu Mag forever. The city in the sky is quite peculiar, but it could never hold my heart like the diamond mountains and crystal leaves of Enu. I feel his body shake as he chuckles against me.

"I like your answer," he says.

"But I didn't give an answer."

"You thought one." He rubs the sweet chill out of my arms. "I know this isn't your thing, baby." He sighs a warm breath against my temple. "I bet I'll turn back into a full vampire when we leave here."

We both look down at his jacket at the same time.

"Is that what you want?" I ask. I feel him shrug against me. I love feeling his gestures.

The silence is filled with his pondering. "You've made a promise that I know you'll keep, and you'll need me for that. As a vampire."

I hook my hands around his neck. I've become

comfortable touching him. In response, his hands cup my breasts, and his thumbs stimulate my nipples.

"Again," I purr, feeling how firm he is against me.

"This is what happens when a guy hasn't wanted to get it on in over two hundred years."

"But you said you had mules—females that liked you. Didn't you have sex with them?"

He takes a long pause. "No."

"Oh," I say, confused.

"They, um… usually…"

"What?" I ask.

"Go down on me."

I'm confused. He chuckles, feeling the change in my body that alerts him of that.

"Your newness turns me on…" he whispers as he pushes his man part between my buttocks.

"Then if I weren't new, you wouldn't want to make love to me?" I reason.

"No."

"Oh," I say passively.

"No, not *no*, I wouldn't want to make love to you if you weren't new. You're beautiful as hell, sexy too, but that's never been a reason to get me going. With you, it's all of it. The newness, the sexiness.

You're brave, loyal. I can trust you. Even that damn water creature trusts you. All of that makes me want to…" He pushes deeper into my buttocks. "All the time. You make me insatiable. Vampire or man."

"Oh," I say again in the same tone.

He laughs at me.

"But what did you mean by 'go down on' you?" I ask.

He sits me down on the edge of the bed, spreads my legs, and guides my back onto the bed. "I'll show you."

He lifts my legs onto each of his shoulders, and his tongue circles my clitoris again. I'm squirming, torn between wanting reprieve and enjoying the most pleasurable sensation I have ever felt. When I look down to see how he's doing it, he's gazing up at me. I feel that pleasurable explosion, and I fall back against the bed, clench the sheets, and cry out.

He's inside me before the sensation subsides. I can't believe that a mere creature can make me feel this way. His head is tilted back, and he easily lifts my hips off the bed to meet him as he slams into me over and over again, going deeper. The fangs are back. Every thrust makes me want to orgasm. Something has changed. I can't stop moaning and gasping, trying to bear the sharp and harmonic sparking.

"Shit!" he grunts, staring at my face. He sweeps me off the bed and holds me tight as he unleashes the loudest growl I have ever heard.

CHEX SAYS HE CAN SMELL FOOD NEARBY. HE TAPS his nose and boasts, "I still have this."

My eyelashes flutter as I sit cross-legged on top of the bed. "You had fangs! I saw them. You were a Selell when we…" I remember he called it something other than "making love," and that definitely was different. It was more carnal and intense.

"Fucked." He winks. "You see the difference?"

"I think so." I drop my face, simpering bashfully.

He takes my chin and lifts my face. "You're going to make me do it to you again, if you keep that up."

"Oh," I hum.

"It sounds like you prefer the vampire," he implies.

I take a moment to ponder the insinuation. "I believe I do." I'm surprised at myself.

His voice rings out in my favorite laugh. "All right, beautiful." He weaves his fingers between mine and guides me into his solid chest. "I have to find a shower." He kisses me quickly.

"How do you take a shower without waterfalls?" I ask.

He tilts his head curiously. "You've never taken a shower in a shower?"

"I have not," I sadly admit.

"Come join me," he says.

We've already figured out how the yellow strip works. We used it to fold the glass away from the window and open the room to the moon. Since Chex is not that far from it, he stretches an arm to touch it.

"Where's the shower?" he asks.

Two parts of the wall slide open to reveal a small chamber. In the middle of the tiny room are three limestone steps that climb up to a round pillar that's encased by glass. Right above it, a light cuts on and illuminates the entire capsule.

"That's our invitation, baby."

We walk toward the contraption. I follow him up the steps and into the capsule, and I gaze up to see thousands of tiny drops of water floating toward us. Our arms, affected by the change in gravity, drift above our head. Even Chex is captivated by how the delightfully warm drops crawl down our fingers, arms, heads, and chests, making their way all the way down to our toes. The liquid feels smooth and refreshing on my skin. I look at Chex. By the look on his face, he's just as intrigued by the "shower" as I am.

After the last bit of water washes past our feet and disappears, we beam at each other before erupting in laughter. What an unexpected surprise! But we turn quiet when racks with garments materialize along the walls.

"The *nonum'toks*," I whisper. "They've brought garments."

He narrows an eye at me. I give him a tiny smile because he's the one who's new now. He smiles back because he knows exactly what I'm thinking.

"They take care of the House of Benel," I say, answering his look.

"And what are they again?"

"Nonum'toks."

"Are they humans, water people, flying shadows?" he asks.

"They're more like humans."

"Like humans?"

"Yes." I don't know any other way to explain

them. The nonum'toks are fashioned out of the stars of Earth.

"And they bring you clothes?"

"And food," I add. "They take care of us."

"So they're your servants."

"They're not slaves," I say, disgusted by the notion. "They desire to care for the house of Felix Benel."

Chex examines me with furrowed eyebrows. I'm sure he will soon voice what he's thinking, and I'm surprised by how eager I am to know.

"What the hell," he whispers and turns to face the clothing hanging from the racks. He steps out of the shower and ambles over to where a number of black trench coats hang. He lifts the cuff of a coat and sniffs it. "How the hell did these get here? This is mine." He narrows his eyes at me.

I'm relieved that his belongings are here. That means that my father approves. Something about Chex remains a mystery to me. No being can walk through a portal and live unless their blood is connected to one of the pacts.

"How did they know where to find this? Nobody finds my shit," Chex says.

I hesitate because he looks so angry. It seems as if he's directing this emotion at me. I try not to take it personally, which would've been easier to do before we made love.

"There is always one who knows where you hide, Chex," I reply.

Suddenly, his frown fades into a wry grin. I've amused him somehow.

"You're not going to get me to believe in that shit," he says snidely.

"I already told you, belief is your choice, not mine." Goodness, I'm being defensive.

He looks away and rifles through the black. He takes a hanger that holds a pair of very black pants off the rack. "My favorite," he says as if I'm not here with him.

Father taught me never to internalize the feelings and emotions of others, especially if I know I've done no wrong, and in this case, I haven't. The nonum'toks brought his belongings out of generosity. If he cannot appreciate that, then it is not my fault. So I decide no longer to dwell on his frustration. I turn away from him to look through the garments that have been reserved for me. There's a pair of navy pants in a stretchy material and a long-sleeved shirt, also stretchy. I've never seen anything like these garments, but they appeal to my eyes. I even like how the material feels against my hand and then my arm.

"Hey you," Chex calls. He no longer sounds harsh, so I look at him. He steps over to where I stand and says, "I was just an asshole, wasn't I?"

"An 'asshole'?"

"Rude," he clarifies without being condescending.

"No," I croak because of the way he's staring into my eyes. "You were just expressing what you felt."

"Ad'ru, I was being an asshole," he says. "I don't like speaking to you that way, and I'll never do it again. I promise you."

He lowers his lips to mine, then his tongue is in my mouth. Our kissing is slow and passionate. I whimper in his embrace, and he whimpers too. He tears his mouth away from mine.

"You should get dressed now," he breathes and speeds out of the room, clutching his favorite pair of trousers and a black shirt.

Loneliness joins me after he's gone. I can certainly conclude that I do not like this feeling. Without delay, I put on the pants. They cling to me like a second skin. Then I slip into the shirt. There's a shelf inside it that holds my breasts firmly in place. I jump to test its resolve and then shake my shoulders—my breasts barely move. I can't stop myself from grinning. The pants even have pockets on the hips and the buttocks. I've grown to like pockets. They're quite practical when needed.

I bend over to pick up an odd-looking pair of boots. They're navy on the outside and lined with furry black fibers on the inside. The shaft extends to my knee, and after I slip them on, the long part tightens snugly around my legs. I wiggle my toes. They're encased but comfortable, and so are the pants and the shirt. Everything I'm wearing is sufficient.

Chex's eyes widen when I walk onto an outside patio. He's sitting on a white marble chair at a table formed of the same material. The ci'ke, ton'rek, and ci'cha are displayed on a silver plate. The sight of him and the fruit from the Garden of Naught causes tears to glaze my eyes. Mother knew this day would come. She knew I wouldn't celebrate the Tilt on dut west. But could she have known that I would become this? I look down to examine myself.

"Wow," Chex whispers.

I rush over to join him at the table, but he hurries out of his seat to take me in his arms. He kisses me before I can sit. The sweet juice of the ci'cha coats his tongue. I moan, savoring the familiar taste. Until now, I never thought the ci'cha would become my favorite fruit.

"Yeah, that's some really good stuff over there." He points his chin toward the table and runs a hand through my hair. "Or it could be because I haven't eaten food in five hundred years. Are you hungry?"

I take a moment to assess how I feel. "Strangely, no." All of a sudden, something baffles me. "Chex, you're eating the fruit from the Garden of Naught, which is in Enu!"

"The Garden of Naught? That sounds scary." He searches my face, seeking a contradiction to his statement.

"The Garden of Naught was planted in Enu by our grandmother, Zillael."

"Wait. Don't you have a sister named Zillael?"

"Yes, I do. She was named after our grand-mother." The thought makes me smile. "The Garden of Naught is supposed to bloom forever when the seven sisters join hands in it. But the fruit is only meant to be consumed by us. The fruit nour-ishes and strengthens us in ways that aren't even known to ourselves. Even the Enuians become ravaged by illness if they eat from the Forest. If any other creature consumes the ci'ke, ci'cha, and ton'rek, it will kill them."

He lifts an eyebrow. "So I should be dead?"

"But you're not." I take a moment to think. "It's strange that you are regaining some of your Selell traits, and you're still hungry?"

He nods. "I guess so."

"This is all very remarkable. Don't you agree?"

"I do agree."

Somehow I feel as though there's a double meaning in his reply that's linked to him growing firm against me. We stare into each other's eyes. It's apparent his sexual desire for me has returned. After a moment, he runs his hand down the side of my face.

"I've never seen eyes like yours on another person," he whispers. "They're pure emerald, like the stone."

"Are they?" I croak. My body is responding to his signals.

"But what the hell are you, Ad'ru?" He's staring at me as if he's trying to figure out the answer to his question.

"I am of the beings of Heaven," I whisper, completely under his spell. "And of Enu, and lastly of Earth. Our mother is Ce'lah'ime, and our father is Felix Benel."

"Why do you all look alike? That's strange, you know?"

"I don't know. We just do. My father once said that humans were once conceived in the same way we were, but they have been separated because of their natural inclination toward idolatry."

Chex grunts. "You keep talking like that, and I just might believe you." He snarls and takes a long, thoughtful pause. "Everything that's wrong with humans is because they worship every damn thing in the world. Money, men, books, animals, even wood and shit. They're even worse when they do it in the name of your Creator. They're stupid and don't even realize it's all been done before. Before their new gods came along, there were old ones. The same shit, a different day, a different name, a different book. There's always a damn book."

I cup his chin and kiss his lips tenderly. I now understand his affliction. He has lived too many lives on Earth. Man's greatest weakness has made him bitter.

"Hey," he whispers with his lips so close to mine. "Will you ever have to go back to this place called Enu, and… be done with me?"

I sigh gravely. It's time for the truth. "I have a choice. You're not my bond, which means that you cannot enter the universe of my mother…" I hesitate because I'm not sure my words are true; after all, he was able to enter the portal. "But I choose you, Chex."

"I choose you too, Ad'ru," he declares.

I'm lifted off my feet, and he carts me back to the room with the bed. I taste the ci'cha in his mouth. Its juices combined with his are sufficient to reinvigorate me.

NAVI

The three Ugu Mags get out of the elevator after us. Mag Star stays a step ahead of me, and they follow us as we walk through a gray tunnel with a line of recessed lighting streaking down the middle of the ceiling. I'm still concerned about what she last said to me. What does she think I'm hiding? How does she know that I'm hiding it? But what's more agitating is that I don't like being followed so closely by strangers, especially since I have no idea what's really going on here.

"Is this a trap?" I blurt out when we get to another door with one of those yellow glass strips next to it. Yes, it was a stupid question, but I'll assess how she answers it. No one has ever come out and said, "Yes, it's a trap!" But in a fragment of a second, if I watch very closely, I can see the truth right before they lie.

"It's not a trap," Mag Star says as she puts two fingers on the glass.

I thumb over my shoulder. "Then why the hell are they following us?"

"They're simply going home, Navi."

The steel door slides up, and we all walk through and onto what resembles a white, block-shaped polyurethane platform. This is a transport station of some sort. There are road rails to both sides of us with one razor-thin track running through the middle of them. This is certainly not a train or bus station or an airport. There's no roof above us, only billions of kets and the vibrant moon.

"What is this?" I ask, my mouth parted in awe.

"This is the transition liaison."

"And where are we transitioning to…?"

The three humans in scrubs have already walked past us. Mag Star directs my attention toward them. They step into another elevator, but instead of the door closing, the cube whips around, and just like that, they're gone.

"Where did they go?" I ask, flustered by their sudden disappearance.

I follow Mag Star's answering gaze to the landing strip to my left. One by one, the humans of this universe fly past us, completely naked and lying on top of white mattresses in egg-shaped balls of glass, which glide past us on the single-blade track.

"Are we next?" I ask, amazed by the amount of fear that floods me. The last time I ventured into the unknown, a tree ended up feeding on my blood. "Do I need to call Adore? I don't want to be separated from her for too long." My voice doesn't mask how nervous I am.

"She'll be able to use the portal in the House of Benel to arrive at where we're going." She faces me, and her expression is filled with sincerity. "Don't be afraid, Navi. I know what you've been through. I'm not deceiving you." She makes sure we have eye contact, and she lowers her voice. "What you have, you'll need to use it for more than what you know."

I blink hard. "The medallion?" I ask to test whether she really knows what I've been hiding.

"The medallion," she confirms.

I am dazed and can hardly hear when she tells me to prepare to descend. The ground gives out beneath my feet, and for the third time since I arrived in Dag, gravity carries me down. My heart pounds. I'm so disturbed at the thought of Mag Star having the medallion that I'm barely able to process that not one light shines in the landscape below. What I can discern in the darkness is mostly hills, woods, and lakes that are glistening in the lights of night. I make a gentle landing at the knees of the loblolly pine trees that grow here. This is certainly a forest, and the air smells sweet, like recent rainfall.

"This way," Mag Star says.

We trek up a trail. I'm used to walking in the dark; the dangers of doing it have sharpened my instincts. In my experience, something grisly is always lurking in the brush. But not here, not now.

"This is a big difference from where we left," I say to interrupt the sound of our footsteps.

"This is Candunk, the fragrant forest."

"Ah." I breathe deeply, more enlightened now. "A concoction of sassafras and rain. You grow Earth plants here."

"Oh yes! Our universe is the spitting image of Earth. The only difference is that we take special measures to preserve the sanctity of our lands, seas, and skies."

"But you've built cities in the sky—that can't be too safe."

"The city is safe," she replies. "The materials we build with are not manufactured. They are mended from natural resources. Our energy is lunar and solar, and we only use it for what's essential in life."

"Is that how you came to know about my medallion, by using your energies for the essentials of life?"

She glances over her shoulder to glare at me. Well, that's refreshing—the Ugu Mag can feel anger. The slope we're climbing tables off.

"Stand there." Mag Star points at one of two white circles that hover above the ground.

I climb on one, and she steps on the other. The circles glow, and next, we take a plunge. Down we go, dropping into a raw limestone cave. The circles' innovative use of gravity keeps us from splashing into the pool rippling beneath us. We stop in front of an entrance to a vertical, nature-made cave. We walk into the middle of a chamber that's surrounded by empty, cloudy space.

"This is the hub," Mag Star says.

"The hub of what?" I ask, openly mocking what I see as a little of nothing.

She struts confidently to a platform. As soon as she touches it, tiny wires snake up and attach to her temples. Two curl over her head and attach to the nape of her neck, and two more go to the top of her skull.

Suddenly, live parts of Manhattan, *Chan'kel* on Ir, the Tree of Life on Jari, and the Forest of Naught on Enu materialize in the emptiness. Other universes also appear—even the sticks of Deadget in Siffeo. That's where I stole the medallion that's the size of my palm, coated with pure gold from the core of the ruby mountain that the Ritkeo worship nonstop. It takes the gold from the ruby mountains to contain the power inside the medallion.

"Do you have it?" she asks.

I dig into my pocket to retrieve it. I can't feel it, so I search harder. "It's not here!"

"You're looking for this?" Mag Star unfolds her balled-up hand. There it is, sitting on her palm.

"How did you get that?" I shout. I'm tempted to snatch it out of her hand and run. But I don't want to put Adore's life in jeopardy, and I remember what she said—with the medallion, she can help us get what we want.

"It's made of evil. I retrieved it before you entered Dag." She curls her fingers back around the object. "I know why you need this."

I study her face, searching for truth. How could she know? "Why?"

"This."

A red haze pours over the environments beyond the platform. A dust storm blows, and up high, like a bright dot, there's the sun. People sit in large groups, huddled close and trying to protect themselves from the sand that the wind uses to whip them. I can't begin to guess where this place is or who those people are.

"It's Tetra," she says.

I flinch, taken aback. "That cannot be Tetra. Tetra doesn't have a sun or humans!" Just to be sure, my eyes find the sun again.

"You are correct. A sun is not native to Tetra. And those are not humans—they're vampires."

I frown, extremely confused. "Vampires can't survive in the sun."

"Their flesh burns hot, but they are not destroyed. What they are experiencing is pain, a torture that no creature should endure. She's there," Mag Star says. "The one you agreed to free."

I swallow the lump in my throat. "Gia Scoralini?"

She slowly turns to face me. After a long moment, she narrows her eyes. "Yes."

"Then you know"—I point at the medallion in her hand—"that I need that to get her out of there?"

"Yes," she replies.

"You're aware that I've been lying to my sister."

"Yes." She sounds satisfied by my admission. "If you had told her the truth, do think you'd be here, at this place, at this moment?"

I sigh, exasperated. The truth is, I don't know, but surely it is time to find out. "You said there's a portal?"

Mag Star nods and returns to her post. I close my eyes and call for Adore.

CHAPTER 9

THE RESCUE
ADORE

N a'ta glares at me. "Why didn't you come as soon as Mag Star opened the portal for you?"

Chex followed me into a wide-open chamber. I'm too mesmerized by the sight of thousands upon thousands of beings being battered by the strong winds to respond to Na'ta. My feet move me forward of their own volition. Before I can reach the edge of the floor, Chex is behind me and holds me by the waist to keep me from getting any closer. I hear Na'ta blow an exaggerated sigh.

"Is this Tetra?" I ask. "The abyss of those who were once Selells?"

"Can you take your hands off of her already?" Na'ta blurts out, unable to contain her agitation.

"What's your problem?" Chex roars and plants his hands tighter on my waist, refusing to abide by her wishes.

"Yes," Magnificent Star says loudly to claim all of our attention.

I whip my face around to see her standing behind a pillar. Wires stream out of her head, and it takes me a moment to realize that she's not hurt. She's somehow manipulating the environment beyond the floor. The wires withdraw from her head, and she walks toward me, carrying something. Na'ta sees the object and tenses.

"You're going to need this." Magnificent Star takes my hand and presses a round, flat piece of gold against my palm.

I run a finger across it. I'm stung by the power of evil inside it.

"Navi, do you want to tell her what it does?" she asks Na'ta.

Na'ta swallows hard. She pulls her mouth tightly to gnaw on her bottom and then top lips. She only does that when she's extremely nervous—which is hardly ever. Immediately I know she never intended for me to find out about the object in my hand. I focus on her face as I step out of Chex's arms. We know each other very well, my sister and

I. She knows that I won't look away or let the matter drop until she tells me the truth.

"We can revive one soul in Tetra with that," she says, pointing toward my hand.

"You mean take a vampire out of torment?" Chex's voice booms so loudly that it echoes throughout this cave.

Na'ta vacillates. Her first instinct is to ignore him because she dislikes him for loving me, but she owes me the truth. She sighs hard. "One vampire. Gia Scoralini."

"No!" Chex shouts even louder. "You'll keep that witch in hell if you know what's good for—" He smashes his lips together. "You'll take her out of there over my dead body."

"Fine," Na'ta hisses with a snarl, challenging him.

"I'm afraid he's right, Adore," Magnificent Star states calmly. "She's a siren. She bewitches and devours men, and vampires, for sport, especially the sons of Gogulon." She looks at Na'ta in a forceful way. "Telman didn't go into Siffeo with you, did he?"

Na'ta shuts her eyes tightly and shakes her head. "Sorry, Adore. I didn't want to lie to you."

She looks so pathetic that I reach for her hands,

filling her with comfort. "You never have to lie to me, Na'ta."

She nods frenetically. "Yes, I did. This Gia craves the love of our Selells, and she won't rest until she has one for herself."

"Ze Feldis is the one she'll kill to claim," Chex says.

Magnificent Star says, "Chex, you still haven't figured out that the blood of Gogulon *is* pumping through your heart?"

He appears genuinely bothered by the revelation. Na'ta and I look at each other. I think we've both been wondering how he could enter the portal and survive. Now we know.

Although I'm rattled by this revelation about Chex, I still have questions regarding Na'ta's motives. "Na'ta, where is Telman?"

She sighs as if the answer causes her much stress. "Exgesis has taken him and hidden him so deep that I can't find him. I was out of options."

"You were not out of options," I snap. "As Father says—you're not an island. You could've come to me, and I would have directed you to our other sisters."

She just raises her hands with a sigh, a gesture of

hers that I've seen time and time again. As usual, she's right—to quote her, "Would've, should've, could've, but there's no way of going back and changing it now."

"The medallion is a blessing and a curse," Magnificent Star says. "It will allow you to go through Tetra and into Ol, which is the fastest and safest way, but you'll be unable to keep Gia from following you into Ol. That will free her to return to Earth if she chooses."

"No worries," Chex says, a violent intention behind that look in his eyes. "I'll send her back to where she belongs, sooner or later."

I relish in the satisfaction of, for once, seeing Na'ta look at the Selell I love with a glint of appreciation in her eyes.

"So Exgesis wanted you to free Gia *and* force us to retrieve the Scepter of Gant?" I ponder aloud, trying to put together the pieces of this extraordinary puzzle. "If he's bonded to me, then he knows that your predicament with Telman isn't enough to force me simply to hand the scepter over to him."

"True." Na'ta pulls her eyebrows together as she contemplates. "He has Telman. I'll do whatever it takes to save him. But..." She studies Chex and then looks at me. "Adore, you may be double-bonded."

I grimace.

"What would you do for Chex?" she asks. "Would you go against your ethics? Would you strengthen the evil? Would you free the likes of Gia Scoralini to save him?"

I hesitate, although I must admit that my new circumstances have me confused about what I'm inclined to do, or not do, for Chex. "Is Gia evil?"

"She's crafty as hell," he replies. "She's where she belongs." He's visibly agitated by Na'ta's questions and losing his patience.

I look from Na'ta, to Magnificent Star, then settle on Chex's face. I close my eyes and sigh gravely. "Yes," I admit. "If I were uncertain about his safety, then I would do what I must to release Gia Scoralini back onto Earth, even if she is crafty."

In a flash, Chex curls a hand around my waist and draws me into him. I stare into his incensed eyes.

"That was a hypothetical. In real life, don't ever do that," he growls through clenched teeth. "There's no way Exgesis or his scallywags can get their hands on me, here or on Earth. So there'll be no freeing of *me*."

He clearly finds the mere thought of needing to be rescued insulting. Yet I am not offended. I have determined that Chex has never depended on anyone but himself. He believes there is no force stronger than himself, and if there is one, he will die happily by its hand rather than be subdued by it.

I'm still studying him askance as my thoughts return to what Na'ta asked. "A double bond…" That would certainly explain the powerful feelings I have for him and, I sadly admit, for Lario Exgesis.

"It's almost time to enter Ol," Magnificent Star says. She looks out into the sand storm. "This is the east of Tetra."

"But how could that be?" I ask, gaping at the sun hanging high in the sky. "Tetra doesn't have a sun."

"It's the earth's sun," she replies. "It was brought to Tetra by the power of the daughters of Benel."

I remember what Lario Exgesis told me about the sun disappearing from the earth. He didn't tell me where it had gone. "But why was it brought here?"

"Unfortunately, I do not know the answer."

Chex steps up next to me. His eyes, like Na'ta's and mine, are pinned to the miserable Selells being battered by the elements. It seems the wind is too strong for them to stand in, and the air is too hot to breathe. They are not souls like deceased Selells. They still have flesh and bone.

"Those are second-generation vampires. Last I heard, your sisters got rid of them. So this is where they went," he says as if that's the answer he's been longing to know. "Not dead." He sounds disappointed.

"But why the sun? I don't understand why Cl'auta would call the sun from the earth and send it to Tetra." I know it was her decision to do this, and there has to be a reason why she did. She has the full power of the mind. It also explains why she did not answer when I called. Is she in distress? Is the earth in distress? I turn to Chex. "You said second-generation vampires. What do you mean by that?"

"When Exgesis started making vampires after he was turned back from being a human," Chex snarls, "he made a type that could suck out a human's soul. But here's the deal." He pauses to impart the gravity of what he's about to reveal.

"You kill one of the vampires, and Exgesis acquires the soul."

"What the hell do you mean by 'acquires the soul'?" Na'ta asks.

"You kill him, and Exgesis comes back to life." He points his chin at the vampires. "Somehow, their lives are attached to him. At least that's how it used to be. I'm not sure if it's the same if they're in Tetra."

I'm struck by illumination. "The leaf." I sigh with dread, remembering. "Falu fed him the leaf from the Tree of Life."

My heart is heavy. Lario Exgesis has used his powers to perform the ultimate act of evil—he has taken what was made of God and transformed it to serve himself. It's for this reason that my time has come. Only I, his bond, can punish Lario Exgesis for what he has done. I know what I must do. Lario Exgesis's actions have determined his fate.

"I need to find him," I say through my clenched teeth. I am angry—angrier than I have ever been in my existence.

"You will find him, but first, the scepter," Magnificent Star reminds us. There's a sense of urgency in her tone.

She's right, of course. I mustn't allow my emotions to steer me away from what's important, and that is retrieving the Scepter of Gant and returning it to its rightful owners, whoever they may be. One thing is for certain—we, the daughters of Felix Benel, cannot keep it unless the Mtknv give it to us.

"The earth's sun will also follow you into Ol, and Tetra will once again be dark," Magnificent Star says. "That means Ol will be light, and you'll have sixteen minutes to get inside the Tarantula and take the scepter before all of Ol pursues you. You will not survive that kind of attack. So you'll have to hurry—get in and get out." She directs her attention to Na'ta. "You'll have to carry Adore to the Tarantula." She puts her eyes back on me. "Adore, use the medallion to open the door. You'll need the light in your sight to find the keyhole. It will be on the claw of the front right leg of the Tarantula."

"She's faster than I am," Chex says, meaning Na'ta. "How long will it take me to get there on my own?"

"You'll never make it," Magnificent Star replies casually.

Chex moves close behind me as if he's on the verge of seizing me. "Then she's not going. Not without me." He throws up a hand, halting Na'ta before she can object. "I know… She doesn't need me; she has you. But I can't let her go without me. It's as simple as that."

"Not your choice," Na'ta snaps.

"*Is* my choice," he insists. "And it's no."

"Okay," Magnificent Star says loudly enough to command our full attention. She's getting weary of their back and forth. "You all must agree, and I can present another option."

"What is it?" Chex barks. He still has a tight hold on me.

"You can retrieve Telman, and he can carry you into Ol alongside Navi."

"You have no objections to that, do you?" Chex asks, glaring at Na'ta.

Na'ta's expression is wide. "How?" she says, choked up.

Magnificent Star walks across the floor. We all watch as the wires reattach to her head.

"I was able to follow them this far," she says.

"Them?" Chex asks. "Who are the *them* you're referring to?"

Magnificent Star glances at Chex, then she taps the pillar. He touches my hip before he releases me to stride over to see what she's showing him. His stance is strong, confident. Magnificent Star looks at her handiwork. Tetra has transformed into an Earth city. I know it from the headlights of motor vehicles that blur in the incessant downpour. Humans, dwarfed by cement, stone, and glass buildings, slog up and down the wet sidewalks while holding umbrellas and hugging their big coats.

"Here—Boston, Massachusetts. There were four vampires. They were carrying Telman past the second stoplight, east," she says.

"And then what happened? How did you lose them?" Na'ta asks. Her level of anxiety is heightened.

"Time expired. Time." She sighs gravely. "It's the hub's single flaw. I'm only able to hold a space for nine Earth minutes, and after that, the gateway closes. I can't reopen it for eighteen minutes. When I returned, I was unable to locate them."

Chex grunts and glares at the entire setting, absorbing the cityscape one increment at a time. He's thorough, gazing into the high windows, past the street, and into the depths of the earth. Then he looks at me with a satisfied grin. "I know where they are."

"You have seven minutes, thirty-seven seconds to reach him," Magnificent Star says, but it sounds as if she's posing a question.

"Fair enough." He points at Na'ta and me. "But you two, stay here."

"No." Na'ta's tone is defiant.

"Yes, you will," Chex insists past clenched teeth. "If we had the option to fight all day, then you could come along for the fun of it. Your blood and a vampire's den don't mix. Your coming will be the difference between a scuffle and a war."

"Shit." Na'ta sighs. "You're right."

Chex doesn't take a moment to gloat. Perhaps Na'ta admitting that she's wrong and someone else is right doesn't have the same impact on him as it does on me.

He looks at Magnificent Star. "I just cross that line and I'm there, in Boston?"

She nods. "Yes."

"I'm going to spend five seconds for this…"

Suddenly I'm securely in his embrace, and the familiar taste of his warm tongue caresses mine. I count, *du, dut, duk, du'hi, du'jek, du'te'tu…* My head is spinning. The way he tastes is insanely delicious. *Du' rem'sek*—not in five but in seven seconds, he's gone.

We watch him stride with the confidence of a supreme predator. There aren't very many humans out and about, but they are certainly mindful of his nearness. At first, passersby inspect his remarkable physique, but the longer they look—and they have to look because there's no turning away—their instincts send a warning, causing some to shudder away from his nearness. Others tear their eyes off his splendor, lower their gaze, and hustle past him. But I can't take my eyes off him; I'm mesmerized by his prowess.

With one hand, Chex lifts himself over a high black iron gate. The hub is able to keep a clear eye on him as he moves down the tight opening between the two stone buildings. At the end of the path, he lifts a square cement slab and bounds feet first into the cavity in the ground. He's composed as he free-falls, his arms crossed against his chest, and he lands gently on his toes.

I turn my wide eyes toward Na'ta. She's clearly not as impressed as I am. Her stern eyes are fastened on Chex, and her expression is pensive. I can tell that she's anxious to catch sight of Telman.

A Selell leans against a door at the end of the corridor Chex is stomping down. She has cropped, straw-colored hair, and she's smoking an object called a cigarette. Before she can fully rotate her head to see him, he's in front of her with his hand clamped around her neck. Her lips part, and her eyes widen in horror. Only now do I see what his other hand did—he stabbed her in the heart. He withdraws the blade and is slyly stuffing it back inside his black coat as the Selell collapses on the cement.

Without pausing or creating a stir, he pushes open the door. He spreads his arms, and with a flick of his thumbs, he releases objects from his hands. Then he throws daggers, which fly smoothly through the air. My eyes can hardly keep up with him. Two tiny objects hit the chests of two Selells on opposite sides of the room, and the daggers, four in total, slice the heads clean off four other Selells. One is left standing, and Chex has him pinned against the wall with a forearm against his chest and the tip of a dagger aimed against his neck.

"You're human," Chex growls.

The male is so frightened that he can only nod frantically.

"What are you? A mule or…" Chex takes a whiff. He looks over his shoulder at a table that holds blue powder, glass jugs of liquids, scales, and a sleek, mechanized apparatus. "You're manufacturing zombies?" He sounds disgusted.

The guy just gulps. He's visibly shaking.

"I should kill you." Chex grips the human by the neck.

The man struggles to breathe. My heart is thumping. I don't want him to kill the human. That would be iniquitous.

"He should kill him," Na'ta mutters.

I whip my face around to assess her. She's watching with an impressed sneer. How could she feel such a thing? Isn't it against our nature to crave the death of another? But then I remember Cl'auta and how she desires the death of Lario Exgesis. Either my sisters have developed a trait I do not possess, or they have lost a sensibility I still have.

"But I'm not going to," Chex says, and I sigh with relief. "I'll see you soon" are Chex's last words to the human before the man loses consciousness and collapses.

Chex turns to face another door. His eyes are focused on the metal door as if he can see through it. He waits. The door opens, revealing a Selell, and Chex hits him in the heart with one of the tiny objects. Just for a moment, I take my eyes off Chex to study the face of the dead Selell. His skin has turned thin and chalky, and it clings to the bones of his face. The creature has aged many, many years since his death just seconds ago. Chex skulks down a slanted hallway, making his way deeper into the earth.

"He has two minutes," Magnificent Star announces. I hear the tension in her voice.

Chex spins on his heels. Two, then four, then six daggers spin down the corridor, slicing the heads off their intended targets.

"Holy shit," Na'ta mutters, even more impressed.

Killing does come quite naturally to Chex. I'm not sure how I feel about that, but I will not allow myself to judge him as a barbarian. His actions are necessary. Why can't all universes and their creatures exist in peace like in Enu?

He turns down another corner into a short hallway that leads to a door. This time, Chex uses the heel of his boot to knock down the door. It's clear he's no longer concerned with how much noise he's making.

Suddenly the space beside me feels empty— Na'ta is no longer standing beside me. When I spot her in the room with Chex, I'm slammed by a host of emotions. I'm angry, afraid, and hopeful, but mostly anxious. I can never count on her to follow the plan—she does what she wants, when she wants, without considering the repercussions.

The room is far from empty. It is full of creatures with sharp teeth, pointy ears, and rubbery gray skin. They aren't human, but they have legs and arms and the physical builds of humans. I gasp and press a hand against my heart when I see Telman lying on a thin wooden platform. One of those strange creatures is sinking its teeth into his neck and another has its teeth in the inside of his thigh. However, Telman isn't the only Selell they're feeding on. There are lots of them.

Now that Na'ta is there, not only are the rodent-like creatures riled up, but so are the weakened Selells. Chex isn't happy to see her.

For one long second, all eyes in the room focus on her. The smell of her blood fuels their thirst, and all at once, almost every creature present—except for Telman and Chex—decide to pounce on her. But she's quick and itching to get in on the fight. All that I can see of her is the glare of her long blade slicing through the room. The creatures have gone insane in their quest to seize her, and they're racing into what is certain death.

More Selells race into the dingy space. Chex and Na'ta seem engaged in an endless battle with Selells, because the rodent-like creatures are all dead. Their bleeding bodies on the concrete are a morbid sight. Telman is so weak that he's crawling over the dead, heading toward the open door. He doesn't know that he's being rescued. Then the worst happens.

I wish my eyes were deceiving me. A Selell has caught Na'ta. He's twice her size, and his teeth are deep in her neck. Another Selell kicks the first one in the head and tears Na'ta out of his arms. A new set of teeth are in her neck. She's wobbling, dazed, and Chex is too preoccupied to get to her fast enough. When two Selells swipe Telman off the ground, I know what I must do.

"Thirty seconds," Magnificent Star announces.

She's looking at me nervously because, like me, she can see that they won't be able to cross over any time soon. In twenty seconds, my sister and Chex will be trapped. Even a warrior like Chex can't fight past all of those thirsty Selells.

One second passes before I cross the line that separates Dag from Earth. I discharge the light, aiming one palm at the Selell who has Na'ta and the other at the two who are trying to carry Telman away. The effect of the light is immediate. My marks go stiff and drop my sister and her Selell.

"Ad'ru, get the hell out!" Chex shouts.

He's near me as I fill the room with light. Every thirsty Selell falls to their knees, shrieking with their hands smashed against their eyes. I'm quite shocked by the way the i'lek'u affects them. But we're not out of jeopardy. An uncountable number of them bang on the walls outside the room. They clamor over each other, trying to cross the threshold, only to be halted by the light.

I can tell that Chex is steaming mad as he holds up Telman. I sweep Na'ta into my arms, and we race to reach the slash of light that's diminishing by the second. We tumble to the floor in Dag.

Magnificent Star lets out a deep sigh of relief as she slumps over and grabs her knees. All four of us have made it back. However, there is no way Na'ta and Telman are fit to go into Ol. Our plans have been thwarted.

CHAPTER 10
BUMPS ON THE ROAD
ADORE

"What the hell is wrong with your sister?" Chex barks so loudly that his voice echoes through the high halls. He has been pacing the pristine floor for a while now.

We've ended up at the cure pod anyway. It's very clinical, like a hospital. The only reason I can make the reference is because Pan'a'tua once ended up in one, and Father had to explain to me why she was there and why it was best that she remained within its confines. Chex and I stand outside the door of the room where Na'ta and Telman are being kept. I insisted that they not be separated. It's best they are together since they'll draw strength from each other.

"I told her what would happen, didn't I?" Chex's eyes are ablaze.

I think he's waiting for me to respond. "Chex." I touch his arm, and he recoils. I frown, confused as to why he would pull away from my touch.

"And you let her get away with bloody murder! I need some air." He stomps off down the long hallway. Without looking back, he touches the yellow strip, steps into an elevator, and when the door slides down, he's out of my sight.

I don't understand why he's so angry with me. I close my eyes and focus on my sister and her Selell. Chex is well; they are not. The reason why Pan'a'tua recovered in the hospital was because Father attended to her there. I know for certain that the Dags cure pods will have no effect on Na'ta. When I walk into the room, she's lying on a table, completely nude under a white sheet. Telman is lying beside her, and he's also naked under the sheet. I touch Na'ta's forehead. She's warm.

"My Ad'ru."

I know the voice, and I instantly catch a breath. When his hand touches my shoulder, I take it and hold on for dear life. "Father." *It's him!*

"I am sorry for letting the Selell deceive you," he says then kisses the back of my hand. He gazes at Na'ta and brushes the side of her cheek with his free hand, spreading flakes of light across her face.

All of a sudden, the blush returns to her cheeks, and she opens her eyes. She sees Father's face first, then mine. "Shit…" She leaps to her feet.

"Navi," he says in a way that signals that he's going to reprimand her. "You have put universes in jeopardy by being selfish. Look at me."

She shamefully lifts her face to look him square in the eyes.

"You have no more chances. Do you understand?" he mutters in anger.

She gazes down at the floor again and nods stiffly.

"Now go. Let the Selell draw strength from you. He'll wake when he catches the scent of your blood. Let him drink, and then all of you return to eat from the fruit of Naught." Father turns his pointed glare on me. "Find your Selell and speak to him, Ad'ru."

"Speak to him about what?" I'm confused. What sort of conversation should Chex and I have that Father would deem so important?

He doesn't look so angry. "About how he feels, Ad'ru." His gaze moves between Na'ta and me. "You both are on the verge of failing. Even the flowers grow, daughters, and so must you." He slices the air with his hand, and there at his beck and call is a portal. "The Scepter of Gant—I want it in your possession. Do you understand?"

"Even if it doesn't belong to us?" I ask.

"It does belong to you."

"Not if we steal it from the Mtknv."

"Then don't."

Na'ta and I are motionless as we watch him disappear through the portal. We remain silent for a while.

"Is Chex angry with me?" she asks.

I nod.

She sighs gravely and shakes her head. "He should be. I screwed up." She looks at Telman. Her voice cracks as she says, "We almost lost him."

We both study him. He doesn't look the same lying there with his eyes closed and his skin deathly pale. When he's awake and vibrant, his eyes are pale blue, lighter than the Enuian sky, and his mouth is very red. Unlike Chex, Telman has a soft appearance. But now he just looks... empty. Na'ta slides off the table and walks to his side. She bends over to kiss his lower lip as she smooths his light-brown hair with her hand.

"Telman, wake up," she whispers. "It's me." She slides her neck on his lips. "Drink. It's me…"

I'm caught in curiosity as Telman stirs. His fangs slowly grow. Na'ta pushes her neck against their sharpness. I jump with a gasp when they pierce her skin. This is the first time I've seen a bond drink from a lifeblood. Only recently did I learn that this was even possible. He takes her by the hair and flips himself on top of her. They're both on the tabletop, and she's breathing heavily.

I recognize the sounds they are making—the same noises Chex and I made when we were making love. I cannot watch Na'ta engage in such an act, so I turn my back on them and speed out of the door as fast as my Enuian and celestial parts can carry me. Once I'm in the hallway, I feel relieved to have escaped Na'ta and Telman's moment of passion, but there is still no sign of Chex. I remember what Father advised me to do. I must find him, although I am content to let him resolve his own dilemma. Surely that would be the wisest decision.

I adhere to Father's counsel, however. I find Chex easily as he's made his way back to Father's dorm. When I enter through the wide-open window, he's sitting on the strange, energy-molded sofa. He looks like a foreign object in the room, sitting rigid and grim-faced. He stands and parts his lips as if to speak, but he doesn't.

"I don't understand why you're angry with me," I confess, thinking that's the best place to start.

"What I did, what do you think about it?"

"The killing?"

He snorts cynically. "No clarification needed."

"I don't think anything," I say after gauging my feelings.

"Sure, you do!" he roars.

"I do not purport to tell *you* how you feel, and you should not do the same to me."

"See that," he says, pointing at me. "You're like a robot. You can turn yourself off and on, and shit, Ad'ru, I can't live like that!"

"I'm sorry, Chex, but your words are not cohesive. At first you believe that I'm offended because you feel I've judged you for killing, and now you're upset because I'm dispassionate. And both of your accusations are wrong."

We stand looking at each other, assessing each other. I'm still unable to figure out what is troubling him so.

Then he asks, "If I was to go to the hub and tell

Magnificent Star to get me the hell out of here, how would you feel about that?"

"Upset, hurt…" I answer.

"Yeah, but for how long?"

I walk over to him and take one of his hands. "Chex, it is not that I wouldn't miss you and think of you during every moment under the Enu sun." I freely smooth a finger along his lower lip. "It is not that I wouldn't crave your kiss, your touch, your body against mine, or to hear your voice. But if you are happier away from me, well then, so be it."

"What about the killing?" he breathes; there's desperation in his voice.

"I know that you are a warrior of the blood of Gogulon. The power to judge is a heavy burden to carry, and it's not mine or yours or any being's— only the Creator's."

I think he mutters the F-word before he smashes his lips against mine. He's no longer angry with me. Apparently I've said the right things because his man part has grown firm against me.

"I'm never going to leave you, Ad'ru," his warm lips whisper against mine. "I want you to know…" His eyes close, his breaths heavy, and his forehead presses against mine. "I will kill Exgesis, even against your wishes, if he tries to take you away from me."

I don't tell him what I already know. It's too risky. The truth is, when I'm done with Lario Exgesis, he will no longer be a threat to our bond. So I was not completely truthful with Chex. Lario Exgesis is the one creature I will pronounce judgment upon.

Chex's lips, tongue, and sharp fangs ride up and down the side of my neck. He is now a full-on Selell. My instinct pleads with me to allow him to drink from me—or perhaps it is my curiosity. I can't get the sight of Telman sinking his teeth into Na'ta out of my head, or the fact that my father encouraged it.

"Do you thirst for me?" I whisper, reeling from the tickle of his mouth.

"In more ways than one." He consumes my earlobe.

I release an unrestrained gasp. "Do you want my blood?"

All of sudden, he stops and looks me in the eyes. His expression asks me if I mean what I ask. I nod.

"Yes," he can only barely say. "Very much."

"Then take it."

"Can I take all of you?"

"Take all of me." I sigh and close my eyes, bracing for his bite.

There's a slight prick, but the rest is like sliding down the Ancient Falls of Enu. My stomach drops. My head is giddy. I'm being lowered onto the sofa, and one of his hands is inside my pants. His fingers slide up and down my female parts. Once he finds that one spot he's so expertly searched out and conquered, he circles it. I'm experiencing so many sensations at once, and they're all powerful and unrelenting.

I feel my lips part and hear myself moan and cry, trying to endure the blasts of pleasure. Chex throws his head back and bellows the loudest growl I have ever heard. I see traces of my blood on his teeth.

"Now I'm going to fuck you," he announces gruffly.

Before I know it, my pants are off. He's standing and holding me against him, shifting my hips as his erection slides in and out of me. There's something wild about how he's doing it this time. He grunts, even when his mouth finds mine. This is the real Chex—brazen, brash, and unrepressed. He's so different from myself, but this is the way I prefer him. After he expends a second very loud chain of growls, he wraps his arms tight around me, squeezing me close.

"Now that we got that out of the way," he says, lightening the mood. "About those bat people... Where the hell did they come from?"

I chuckle into his strong neck while holding tightly to him.

NAVI

I thought I would never hear Telman growling so soon. He's consumed enough of me, and he's released himself. Sex is always a pleasurable experience, but I can live without it. It sucks up too much time, and Telman usually agrees.

"You found me," is the first thing he whispers.

"We," I clarify. "Ad'ru and that vamp Chex."

That gets him up and going. He's standing. "Where are my clothes?" He uses his speed to whip his face around. "Why the hell am I naked anyway?"

"Calm down, vamp. We're in Dag, and to them, naked is natural," I look over my shoulder in the general direction that anybody might be. "Hell, they might have burned our clothes for all I know."

Telman eyes darken with desire as he latches onto my arm and pulls me to him. I slam into his chest, and his tongue is deep in my mouth, almost down my throat—where I like it.

"That took my breath away," he claims breathlessly. "You know what I want, Navi." He chuckles a little, "But you mentioned Chex? That's a dangerous vampire. What the hell is he doing here?"

I can hardly contain myself. Finally, I get to tell someone who will understand that we hit the jackpot. I nuzzle up closer to him, beaming from the inside out. "Get this. He's Adore's bond." I must see Telman's face. Just as I predicted, he's speechless. "I'm not done." I brace myself to tell him this. "So is Exgesis. He's her fucking bond too!"

His amused smirk diminishes into a hard line. I also predicted that reaction.

"Too bad because he's dead," Telman growls.

I snort facetiously. "I don't know if we're first or last in line for that."

"What will Adore think about it?"

I sigh because I care. I've disappointed her enough in my lifetime. After my last fuckup, when the vamps used me like a rag doll, I promised that if I got out alive, I would never do it again. I meant it. "She'll have to agree."

"Not going to happen." Telman sounds as though he has no doubt about that. "Wait. Has she even met Exgesis? Hell! Or Chex?"

"Yeah." I grin and nod, pleased by the irony of the situation. "She's not in Enu anymore. She's here."

His thumb flicks my lower lip. "The sneer. It's sexy."

"Stop, Telman." I'm blushing. "Come on, we're talking shop."

He cocks his head to one side. "Navi, you come on… Is it going to be this bed or does your father have a stash here in Dag?"

"You know him so well." I beam at him. We don't have time for sex, but in this case…screw it. "There's a stash here in Dag."

He follows me down the hallway, out the window, across the skyline of the floating city, and into my father's dorm. I'm hot for him, but I go cold as soon as I see the blue pants crumpled on the floor at the foot of the couch.

"Shit!" I grumble.

"What?" Telman breathes heavily behind me. His hand is running up and down my crotch.

"Ad'ru!" I shout as loud as I can. "Ad'ru!" I'm shaking.

"What's going on?" Telman is still confused as hell.

I throw up my hands. "They're fucking again. I mean, how many times is he going to do her?" I break away from his grasp. "I like that we have Vestop Mallotnis on our side, but hell, why can't he keep his hands off my sister?"

"What did you call me?" Chex appears with only his pants on, standing behind Adore, who's holding the bedsheet around her. He looks genuinely conflicted. "I assume you mean that I can't keep my hands off Ad'ru, but *Vestop Mallotnis*...?"

"You don't remember your name?" I ask him.

"I remember my name. It's Chex. How do you know me as Vestop Mallotnis?" He glares at us as though he wants to slice off our heads.

"I know things, that's all," I say.

He sighs hard, and frustration colors his expression. But Adore gazes up at him and slides a hand through his hair. He rests his forehead on hers.

She's tender with him, and finally I see—it's too late. She loves that dangerous vamp.

ADORE

We've dressed ourselves, and Chex and Telman join Na'ta and me at the table in a room exposed to Dag's new dawn. I feel as if we're mingling with a purple and orange sky. The air is fresh and cool. We're all eating from the Forest of Naught; yes, even the Selells.

"Lario Exgesis took memories from Falu also. I wanted to tell her everything about herself, but Father said no, that she'd find out in due time," I say.

"And what about Ben Artiste?" Na'ta glances at Telman. "For all we know, he fell off the face of the earth."

I'm perplexed, and it shows on my face. "How can you fall off the earth? It's not possible."

The way she sighs signals that I'm once again behaving as if I am *new*. "It's a figure of speech, Adore. It means that he can't be found."

Chex smirks at me, and I bashfully look at my

plate of sliced ci'ke and ton'rek. He lifts my chin as he always does and gazes into my eyes. I feel as if time is standing still. There's a thought behind the way he's beholding me, but it's not lust.

"He's on the earth," Chex announces and tears his eyes away from my face to look at Telman. "He was with Ze Feldis and Elo when I outfitted them with mercury. It was the fastest way of killing a second-generation vampire, short of slicing off their heads."

"Second-generation vampires? What are those?" Telman asks.

Chex snorts, shocked. "You haven't heard of them? They were feeding off of us regular vampires. Wiped out the Olympus coven, Kili-manjaro—"

"That's what? Ten thousand vamps?" Telman exclaims.

"Thirty-seven thousand, five hundred and two, to be exact." Chex scowls curiously. "Where the hell have you been that you didn't know this?"

"Everywhere but the earth. Mainly the kark forest. We've lived there for a while."

No wonder the trees recognized the hymn of gratitude and protected me from the Mtknv. I glance at Na'ta, but she's focused on following the discussion between the two Selells.

"They're no longer an issue, the sisters and their vamps." Telman grins cynically. "Well, I thought they did what was smart and killed them, but they're in Tetra."

There's a short moment of thoughtful silence. We're all very comfortable dining with each other. I catch Na'ta studying my neck. When we lock eyes, she turns quickly to Telman.

"We're going in for the Scepter of Gant," she says to him.

"Is it because we have more firepower this time?" he asks.

"Wait." Chex sounds astonished by what he just heard. "What do you mean by 'this time'? You two tried to take it before?"

"Of course." Na'ta sounds smug. Her top lip is curled in that way that agitates me. I know she's about to do something dangerous whenever she does that. "We heard the Mtknv were raided, so we decided to—"

"Take it back," Telman finishes. "But we almost got ourselves killed. We didn't know they had the eye. They saw us—well, me—coming." He shows the same smug smile Na'ta is displaying. "So we're going back in?"

Out of nowhere, Chex lets out the loudest laugh. Whatever amuses him is not only a mystery to me, but to Na'ta and Telman as well.

"They must drive you nuts, babe," Chex says, rubbing my back. His touch feels divine. "He's just like her!"

I can only shrug, because I can't even begin to verbally convey how true that is. Just as Chex and Na'ta had a shaky beginning, so did Telman and I.

"I make her batshit crazy." Telman laughs before taking one big bite of ci'ke. "But now she loves me, right, Ad'ru?" He winks at me.

"Very much so," I say with a smile. I think I'm blushing. He and I have come a long way.

"I know you want me to keep my hands off of your sister, but it's hard when she does that!" Chex's eyes gleam as he gazes at me.

"Try," Na'ta snaps. "And while you're at it, could you stop calling her 'babe'? It's just… weird."

"Na'ta, silence," I command. "You respect what we have as I respect what you have with Telman."

Chex squeezes my hand. I know it's his way of thanking me for finally defending our love to her.

Na'ta shrugs.

"Yeah, *babe*; Adore has a point," Telman says, surprising me. He normally lets us squabble and pretends as if he's not paying attention.

"Okay, I get it." She points at me. "But you'd better be there when I call you. It's our pact, remember that."

"We'll both be there," Chex says, speaking before I can.

"And vice versa," Telman adds.

"Good." Chex kisses my knuckles. "Now that we've got that out of the way… Telman"—I like how he pronounces his name, like *Telman* is a word in a beautiful song—"you've got speed, and I need you to carry me into Ol with these two." Chex tilts his head toward Na'ta and me.

"You got it," Telman replies without debate. He's so different from Na'ta in that regard. He doesn't like to quarrel.

"One more thing: what about the bat people who were feeding off you? Where the hell did they come from?"

"The blood slugs?"

"Is that what they're called?"

Telman glances at Na'ta. "That's what we call them. They're from the swamps of Glooms. You can take one guess how they got to Earth."

"Exgesis," Chex replies with a disgusted snarl.

"The one and only. As you saw, they like blood. Vampire, human, or animal—it doesn't matter. And they have no cutoff point. They'll drink you dry and do it slow. It hurts like hell." He cringes, recalling the agony. "I was in pain, I begged death to hurry up and get on with it."

"That bastard," Na'ta curses under her breath. "He was going to kill you? That wasn't part of our deal."

Telman snarls like what he's about to say is already leaving a bad taste in his mouth. "Reefer brought me a message from Exgesis before he threw me in with the blood slugs. Exgesis said thanks for getting him what he wanted, but the deal is off because we're not making it easy for him."

"What did he get that he wanted? Isn't Gia still in Tetra?" Chex asks.

"Wait." I close my eyes and sigh gravely. All eyes are on me, waiting for me to reveal what I'm thinking. "Your bargain was to release Gia. That happens if we enter Ol through Tetra, and according to the Aarap and Magnificent Star, that's our safest way in. But not only that, he knew you could get the medallion and we would need it to get into the Tarantula!"

"He set this all up," Chex says.

"So what do we do?" I ask. "Do we give up on our quest?"

"Father said we're supposed to get the scepter," Na'ta reminds me.

"If *Father* said it…" Telman says sarcastically.

Na'ta gives him a look. "Shit," Na'ta hisses under her breath. "I have to contend with Gia Scoralini again." Her scowl intensifies, and Telman turns away from her.

"But you made the deal," I remind her. "You knew you would have to contend with her anyway."

She turns her scowl toward me.

I'm not backing down from her nasty look, but as the holder of the light, I can't help noticing the sudden change in the atmosphere. I quickly turn to look outside. "Look, the sun has fully risen."

Suddenly it's extremely bright out, and the room is heating up. Tinted glass automatically slides down the opened wall.

"This is a strange place," Na'ta mutters, observing the nearly blinding brightness beyond the glass.

"That's why we work in the cities at night," Magnificent Star says.

We all turn to see her standing on the wide threshold of this room.

"The hub is closed until after sundown," she says. "Make yourselves comfortable here, but I advise you not to go out into the city while the sun is up."

I stand. "But we're ready to go into Dag. We can't wait. You must open the gateway for us."

Chex stands beside me. I believe it's in support.

Magnificent Star's eyes dart back and forth between us. "I'm sorry. We do not operate power during daylight."

We all watch in disappointment as Magnificent Star turns her back and exits.

"Let's just finish eating," Telman says and playfully tugs Na'ta's arm. "Then we'll do what we came here to do." He lifts his eyebrows suggestively at her.

A time existed when I wouldn't have understood what he meant. It's difficult to picture Na'ta and Telman engaging in the same acts that Chex and I have engaged in, but I saw a slice of what it may look like at the cure pod.

"Ah," Na'ta says, eyeing me while wearing a wry grin. "You starting to feel my pain, I see."

"What's wrong with you two!" Telman's voice

booms. "You're hot and sexy! You need to be... um..." He circles his hand like a conductor as he searches for the perfect word.

"But I'm not hot," I say. The temperature of the room is perfect.

They all erupt in laughter.

"So, Chex," Na'ta coolly says, grinning at him. Her tone indicates that she's simply changing the subject, and more than that, she's about to probe Chex for information. "Weren't you the one who wiped out Gung-ho?" She winks at Telman.

It appears that he's no longer interested in sex either. He is eager to hear what Chex has to say.

"Maybe." Chex flashes his teeth. "Maybe not."

"Come on, Chex," Na'ta begs while smirking. "I let you poke my sister, don't I?"

"Is that so?" Chex says dismissively.

Telman turns all his attention on me. "These vampires, Adore? There were about fifty of them, and they used to convince impressionable children to give them their blood."

I gasp, horrified.

"But someone wiped them out, and anybody who ever partook in kid-cocktailing—that's what they called it." He turns back to Chex. "Admit it, it was you." He looks back and forth between us. "It'll impress Adore."

"It will?" Chex asks, raising his eyebrows at me in a sultry manner.

I can't help but simper under the power of his gaze.

"Then it's true." His acknowledgement is lackluster.

"I knew it!" Na'ta shouts, pointing at Telman.

For a very long time, Chex, Na'ta, and Telman share stories about all the bad Selells they have encountered. It's funny how they look for commonalities. I remain quiet as I watch and listen. I've never seen Na'ta like this. It seems the more the conversation deepens, the more affectionate she becomes toward Telman.

She nudges Telman in the chest because she's very close to him now. He has his arm around her shoulder. "Felix sent us into the World Bank in Beijing," she says. "We had to get a ring. That's what we do; we recover shit for my father."

I flinch, taken aback. "You do?" I did not expect to hear her say that.

She curses under her breath. She's behaving as if she has made a mistake by divulging the information. Everyone is surprised by my outburst, even

Na'ta, who just watches me with wide eyes but says nothing more. I want her to speak.

"Was that to be a secret?" I ask. "I worry about you all the time. I thought you were living your life carelessly and putting it in danger for fun!"

"Well, then you should calm down, Adore, because I do that too!" She's on the edge of her seat, leaning across the table toward me. "You know what…"

I have awakened the beast. She's ready to spar, and so am I.

"You talk a lot of shit," Na'ta says.

I cringe. "Can you stop saying that? That word makes me uncomfortable."

"Why? You don't even know what it means."

"It means bodily excrement," I say with my teeth clenched. I lean across the table and face off with her.

"Like I was saying, you talk all of that…" She rolls her eyes. "Stuff, but you're judgmental, Adore. You judge me all the time!" She stabs her chest with a finger.

"I don't judge you, Na'ta." I sigh. But then I remember Chex leveling the same accusation against me earlier. I turn to look at him, because I'm out of words.

"Hey." He gently lifts me to my feet. "Let's go rest."

Na'ta watches us with wide eyes. Telman is glaring out the window and shaking his head. He's disappointed that one of our spats ended his conversation with Chex.

"We'll see you at sundown," Chex says as he leads me out of the room. He pulls me down the hall and to our bed. Keeping his eyes on my face, Chex gently pulls off one of my boots, then the other, and guides me down on the bed. He lies behind me and hugs me into him. "Your sister is high voltage."

"I don't know what that means."

He chuckles against me and guides my hair over the front of my shoulder so he can kiss the back of my neck. "It means she sucks up a lot of energy." He pulls me in closer. "She really made you angry, didn't she? I've never seen you worked up like that. I thought you were going to zap her with your light."

I laugh softly, remembering how often I've tried to do that. "She's too quick."

Chex's laugh sounds delicious.

"She's the only sister I'm close to," I say after he falls silent again. Admitting to Chex what I always keep locked inside me is easy. I flip around, and Chex loosens his grip on me so that I can face him.

He kisses me gently and slides his hand down the side of my face.

"But don't be alarmed if we spend too much time together," I say. "We usually, eventually, get to this point. Father says it's because we're fire and ice, except he doesn't know which one of us is the fire or the ice."

We stare into each other's eyes. There's a question I want to ask him, but I'm not sure I should.

"What do you want to know, Ad'ru?"

For a moment, I wonder if he somehow has a power of the mind. I hesitate but ask anyway. "As a human, even a Selell, you have free will. Why have you made the choices that you've made?"

"I've made a lot of choices. Which ones are you referring to?"

I hesitate. "You will not think I'm being critical if I say it?"

"No."

"You've killed a lot of Selells. I realize that they were influenced by the evil and intending to harm others, but you didn't know that you were of Gogulon until recently."

His expression hardens, and I fidget under his

glare. I can see him contemplating whether he should respond to my questions. I'm relieved when he parts his lips to speak.

"My mother was a peasant, and my father was the king. He ordered my death the day I was born, and I've been trying to survive the sword ever since." He reaches over to smooth the crinkle from between my eyebrows. "So many questions, my emerald-eyed beauty." He seems captivated by the way I'm looking at him. "I learned how to kill men in iron suits, men who were twice my size, by the time I was six years old."

"Learn? Who taught you?" I ask.

"My mother was big on fucking, not marrying —she was born way before her time. But she was involved with Remus Maddix. He was the assassin charged by the King to kill me. He was hell-bent on doing just that until he fell into lust with my mother. Because"—he hesitates, and a veil of disgrace shapes his expression—"she was a siren."

Now it's my turn to touch his face and bring him comfort. "Do not be ashamed, Chex. A siren is not created by the ambitions of the ek'et'ru."

He looks even more conflicted as he ponders what I just said. "Well…" He stops to clear the catch in his throat. "Maddix taught me how to fight. When I was six, I killed my first mercenary. I had a boy's strength, but I slayed him because I was faster and smarter."

"And what happened to Remus Maddix?" I ask. I'm utterly enthralled by this story of Chex's past.

"He's still around."

"Is he a…?"

"Vampire? Yes."

I flip onto my back and look at the ceiling. I can't picture Chex as a boy before his first kill, but I can imagine him as a tiny human male, handling a dagger and killing a man. "And what happened to your father, the king?" I turn to look at him.

He studies me curiously. "I didn't kill him, if that's what you think. Actually, I became an assassin for him. He didn't know who I was."

I can't imagine Felix Benel not knowing who I am, or issuing a command to have my sisters or me murdered. Chex's finger smooths out my eyebrows again.

"What are you thinking?" he asks.

"How harsh and barbaric your father was for trying to have you killed."

"You said you didn't judge," he says.

"I do not."

"He wasn't harsh or barbaric, Ad'ru. The rules

that governed him were. Once the Romans called themselves Catholics, sane men became fools."

"Catholicism, that's a religion?"

"The mother of them all."

"Is that why you don't believe in the Creator?"

"Bingo."

"Oh, I see…"

"Hey," he says, grinning, "I don't have to tell you what bingo means!"

I chuckle. "I may be new, but I'm not slow. You've used that word before, and I referenced the context."

"Smart, beautiful, sexy…" He scoots closer to me and slips his hand under my shirt and up my sternum until he's caressing one of my breasts. "And you don't like the word 'shit.' Do you want me to stop saying it? Because I'll try, but shit, your skin is so soft." He lifts my shirt all the way up and sucks gently on the nipple he's already made sensitive. "And when I'm inside you, shit, it feels so damn good," he seductively whispers.

"I like the word," I croak. "Um, when you use it that way."

"That's what I needed to hear, because I can't stop myself from saying it."

"I don't want you to, or Na'ta either. I was

angry with her, and sometimes I say the wrong things when I'm incensed."

"Enough talking."

I look down at myself, because once again, Chex has slipped off my pants at a remarkable speed.

"Take off your shirt," he demands. His eyes regard me with pure lust. Once I'm completely bare, he's on top of me, inside me, pleasuring me. "I'm going to make love to you until the sun comes up." He pushes deeper into me. "I'll fuck you twice another day."

NAVI

Telman growls, and I cry out. I can't deny that this feels insanely good. And since we have to wait until sundown, we do have the time to do it. But I can tell that, just like me, he's itching to get into Ol so we can finally get our hands on that damn scepter.

"Navi," he says as he continues humping me.

"What?" I fight the urge to moan.

"Does Adore know the Scepter of Gant was

stolen"—he grunts with pleasure—"from the Mtknv?"

"Yes." Shit. I'm about to come again.

"She knows we can't give it back?" he asks and grunts. "Under. Any. Circumstances."

"Yes…" I sigh, feeling that damn orgasm working on me.

"She's okay with that?"

"I mean, no!" I cry, and the noise I unleash is way too high for my tastes.

When I stop trembling and open my eyes, Telman's watching me with a satisfied grin. He loves when I lose the battle against an orgasm. My head is always clearer afterward.

"I was thinking…" I whisper, sinking into the mattress.

"You could think through that?"

I chuckle. "Listen, Mag Star said not to go into the city, right?"

He frowns, wondering where I'm going. "That's what I heard." He's still working on top of me.

"Let's just go through it."

"And go where?" he asks breathlessly.

"To the surface." I moan as he shifts his hips faster.

"There's a surface?" he grunts out.

"Yes…" I strain to say.

Telman flips me around, and now I'm on top of him. He's still hard inside me. He grabs my waist as he swiftly moves my hips back and forth. "Then let's go…"

He flips me around again, and now I'm on my knees. He's behind me, pounding the hell out of me. I wrap my arms around his neck and let go, moaning a chorus of *oohs* and *ahs*. I reel from the little orgasms until the big one hits. That's when I lose my mind and cry out at the top of my lungs. He's so damn good at this, and I love the way he grunts and growls with his mouth this close to my ear. He knows I want to hear what I'm doing to him, just like he likes to hear what he's doing to me.

"That was long overdue." I sigh as I drop onto the bed.

He flops down on my back. "Before we go…" He bites me in the neck.

My entire body climaxes as he drinks from me. It only stops when he lifts his face to bellow a growl.

Now we're done.

Telman and I get dressed in a hurry. I hear the faint sound of Chex growling as we walk toward the yellow strip by the window. I figure we'll open it, close it, and hurry to the surface before the heat can fry us. Should be easy.

"Ah," Adore whimpers, singing the universal song of sex.

Really, hearing them getting it on doesn't make me cringe or anything; I don't even care anymore. It's too late to go back to how things were, and I don't think I even want to. I've never gotten Adore out of Enu, and I like having her this close.

"I don't remember this room being empty," Telman says as we walk into what's supposed to be a living room.

"You have to turn the furniture on," I tell him as I shoot over to the yellow strip to show him how to activate the furniture. "There are no set buttons for anything. The module works with the voice and the mind. But I noticed that it counts." I put two fingers on the strip.

"Why would it have to count?"

"When Mag Star put one finger on the glass, she gave it one command and two fingers for two." I put two fingers on it. "Furniture and open window."

We wait in a heightened state of anticipation. Nothing happens.

Telman gives me that "What now?" look.

I try again, but this time, I give it only one command, the most important one. "Open," I say past clenched teeth.

"Where are you going, Na'ta?" Adore asks.

Both Telman and I jump, startled, and turn to see her wearing a pal'k. Chex is shirtless in a pair of black pants. Her cheeks are flushed and her hair messy. They must've stopped in the middle of a passionate moment and gotten dressed in a hurry.

"Out." I feel jittery, as if I've just been caught doing something wrong by Felix Benel. Only it's not him—it's my good and pure, never-does-any-wrong sister.

"But you're not supposed to go out. You'll injure yourself in the heat, and we'll be delayed even longer."

"I'm quick, remember?" I try to control how snippy I sound because I don't want to get into another absurd argument with her.

"I don't understand. Where is your destination?" she asks.

Suddenly I remember—she entered the hub through a portal, not the old-fashioned way I did. "The surface is where the Ugu Mag live, and I can't be cooped up in here a minute longer." I smirk as a thought comes to my head. "And Telman and I don't have the same sexual appetite as you two. I mean, the fucking has got to stop at some point, doesn't it?"

Adore doesn't chuckle at my sarcastic joke, but Chex does.

"What are you going to do when you get there?" Chex says before Adore can ask another patronizing question. It's her way to question me into submission, into admitting my fault and changing my direction. She gets that from Father.

"To the surface?" I say with a smile. I've wanted to explore it ever since hiking through the woods with Mag Star. I just got nothing but good vibes all the way around down there. "You know, go for a swim or something. We don't even have to wear clothes down there." I hope that will inspire Adore to come along. I know how much she hates wearing clothes. An adventure like this may help her get the stick out of her ass.

Chex lifts his eyebrows suggestively at her, and *surprisingly*, she does the same.

CHAPTER II
DAG FUN
ADORE

E ach one of us has tried to open the window by using the yellow panel.

"The only way out is to break the glass," Chex says.

Telman steps up to examine the window. "Is this even glass?" He taps on it and listens to the vibration.

"What about your light, Adore? You can use it to power up things, can't you?" Na'ta asks, ignoring Telman and Chex. She knows that destroying any part of our father's dorm is not an option. She, and I, would rather stay "cooped up" than mar Father's property.

"The i'lek'u does produce electrical currents," I say as I touch the strip. I summon the light to the tips of my fingers and say, "Open." To my relief, the glass rolls up.

The heat immediately overtakes us, and before I can comprehend the intensity of the stifling discomfort, my skin is cooling. I'm fully submerged in water, and then I'm out.

The four of us are drenched as our feet sink into soft grass. The blades are as green as the grass in Enu, and the warm air takes me in its arms. When I close my eyes, I feel as though I'm home. But I can't keep them closed for long, not with a blue lake as bright as the sky fanned out before us. Plopped throughout the water are wispy trees with leaves that appear to flutter on the branches, and a shallow mist rises above the lake. I'm caught in a lingering moment of awe.

"Nice stop, Navi," Telman says, surveying the scene with his eyes narrowed. He tilts his head eastward. "Do you hear that?" He beams at Na'ta with excited, bright-gray eyes.

"I hear it." Chex scowls. He instinctively reaches toward his body, but he isn't wearing his coat or shirt. He sniffs the air twice. "Humans." He frowns, perplexed by his verdict.

"And look." Na'ta points up. We follow where the tip of her finger leads.

A blue satiny substance streaks into the sky, then again in red, orange, yellow, purple, white, and a mixture of other colors. Pretty soon, the sky changes. The multitude of colors paint the atmosphere like a massive sheet swirling over the land. And there's music, string instruments echoing my favorite chords. It has to be a festival, a feast, a celebration!

"Somebody's excited," Na'ta mutters, smirking at me. "Always up for a party."

I feel my mouth pulling into a broad smile. She is right. I love celebrations! I shrink under the power of Chex's adoring gaze. My feet are eager to take me toward the music. There's even a sweet aroma of food roasting. I wonder if the Ugu Mag consume the flesh of beasts. Earth humans do.

"I'll go scope it out," Telman says then glances at Chex and me. "Just to make sure they don't fillet invaders."

Na'ta nods. They work solidly as a team. I have never seen them communicate so efficiently. Usually when I'm with both of them, we are in Enu and Na'ta has returned after antagonizing the sea crea-ture who guards the gates of a buried universe. Of course, I thought she and Telman engaged in such actions for their amusement, but from what Na'ta said earlier, Father sent her into the arms of peril. I'm still confused about why she would choose to keep that from me. Telman is gone, and before we can feel his absence, he's back.

"Oh yeah," he says emphatically. "We should join this fun, but we should leave our clothes right here."

"They really don't wear clothes?" Chex asks, suddenly slightly ambivalent.

"They really don't," Na'ta replies sarcastically. She lifts her arms and turns toward Telman. "Hit me, vamp."

Before I can blink once, she's naked.

Chex turns his head, refusing to look at her. "Wait. You're doing that right here?" He thumbs toward Na'ta. "I see her?" He thumbs toward me now. "And you see her?"

Telman and Na'ta grin at him; they're tickled by Chex's reaction.

"He's already seen her naked a million times," Na'ta says on the tail end of a bitter grunt. "And I'm not putting my clothes back on because you can't take it. I thought you were all into this…"

"We don't have to do this if you're uncomfortable," I say to Chex.

Na'ta lets out a forceful sigh. "It's just my tits

and pussy. You've been looking at Adore's ever since I joined you. And don't worry, Telman had to pick his jaw off the ground the first time he saw Adore and Tapeetha in the raw. Just let your jaw drop. We don't mind."

What she says is true.

"That's not it," Chex barks. "There's nothing about you that turns me on."

"Ouch!" Na'ta says, grinning facetiously. "That doesn't even sting."

"Then what the hell is it?" Telman asks, losing patience.

Chex looks at me. "I don't know; it's respect for Ad'ru."

"Oh, I don't mind. The body is not meant to be covered. I only wear the pal'k when I'm among Earth creatures."

Chex studies me. I wonder what he's searching for. But at the end of his study, he says, "Okay, then let's join them."

I smile and raise my arms like Na'ta did. "My turn."

Chex gives Telman a cautious, side-eyed glance, but he does it. The warm, wet air glazes my bare skin. I haven't felt this free in a long time. After noting how happy I am, Chex kisses me gently.

"Hey, Chex…" Telman shakes his hands, which is his way of asking what in the world Chex is doing. He thinks this is not the time for a kiss.

Telman and Na'ta are not kissers or hand-holders. They rarely watch each other in the same lustful way our other sisters and their bonds gape at each other. I chuckle softly, realizing that I have finally joined their ranks. I have a vampire who lusts for me and I for him. Finally I understand.

When we are all undressed, Na'ta tucks our clothes in a safe place. The grass beneath our feet is sumptuous, like that of a well-tilled valley, and the trees are bushy and abundant. The winged fowls whistle and squawk from the branches, and in the distance, my eyes behold their first primate. I come to a stop. The primate and I observe each other curiously.

"Go on," Chex tells Na'ta and Telman. "We'll catch up."

I can't see Na'ta's reaction, but I feel it. She's not happy about leaving me behind, but she streaks off with Telman. Chex steps up beside me and curls his arm around my waist. That's when the creature jumps, flailing its bony, hairy brown arms while warning me in throaty coots.

"It's saying 'blood drinker,'" I translate.

"You can understand the chimp?" Chex's tone rings curiously.

"Yes…" I'm barely audible because I'm just as surprised as he is. "*Rek tek con'um lek'um*," I call in Enuian.

"What did you just say?" Chex asks without taking his eyes off the primate.

The primate coos again.

"I told him that I let you drink my blood."

"What's he saying now?"

"He wants to greet me, but he can't if you're close. He says you're a predator."

"Smart animal," Chex mumbles.

I believe I hear sadness deep in his tone.

The primate springs up into a tree and hops from one branch to another. We watch it until it journeys out of our sight.

"What would you have done if I wasn't here to interfere with you and the chimp?" Chex asks, grinning.

I detect that he is being humorous. I gaze far off as my fantasies paint pictures in my head. "I think we would've played."

"Played? How?"

"In the trees." I turn to see that his grin has enlarged.

"Is that what you do in Enu all day long? Play?"

"Yes."

"You're shitting me, right?"

"If you're asking if I'm being truthful, then yes. I swim the seas, climb the mountains, explore the forests, caves, valleys, and all the other hidden gems of our land." I sigh nostalgically. "That was my life. Before…"

"Me," he says quietly.

"Before the moment I was beguiled out of my universe."

The silence holds the voices of so many types of birds. I always wished there were animals and insects in Enu. Sometimes the Weks take the form of both, but they are not the actual beings.

Chex draws me into him and presses his forehead against mine. "So she can talk to chimps and likes to play." His gaze seeps deeper into my eyes. His man part is growing against me. "Sorry, but that turns me on… Ad'ru?"

"What is it?" I'm concerned about whatever might be troubling him.

"I want to play with you," he whispers through heavy breathing.

I look up as more colors drift across the sky. As the light of the sun reflects through the sheer hues, it paints colors on our skin. I'm so eager to see more, but Chex's lips and tongue are sliding down the side of my neck and down my collarbone until one of my nipples is warmed by his wet mouth.

My body quivers. "But shouldn't we join..." A piercing moan escapes me as his fang gently stimulates the tip, sending a tingle down my thighs.

All of a sudden, I'm lying on the grass. The blades are as cushiony as a bed of air poppies. His kisses and nibbles trickle down to my female parts, and when he finds that familiar spot and spreads my legs, I know we're not going anywhere soon.

"Shit, you're so soft," he whispers before his tongue circles around my clitoris.

I have nothing to hold on to. I cannot let my fingers rake the grass. I whimper and whine, and he offers no reprieve. Through my heavy panting and squeals, I barely hear him comment on how good I taste and beg me not to come yet because he loves when I squirm. But I can't hold off. I push the back of my head hard against the grass. I open my mouth, and my cry echoes through the trees.

"On your knees," he commands.

My legs are still shivering, and he's already lost patience. Unable to wait until I can get in position, he flips me over. In the next moment, I'm on all fours. He lays on top of my back while holding me firm against him with the one arm curved around my belly.

"I'm going to fuck you twice," he whispers.

Now he's inside me, shifting his man part in and out of me so fast that I can hardly stand the pleasure. I certainly will have to wait to see what's beyond the woods.

NAVI

"Vestop has a high sex drive, doesn't he?" Telman asks while searching over his shoulder. Like me, he was expecting them to follow us, but they're clearly not joining us any time soon.

I force a hard breath out of my nose. "Don't all you vampires? If I didn't put the brakes on you, you'd fuck me into oblivion. Because there's no way I can refuse you when you get me going."

"You'd better change your attitude, or I'll put these fingers on you." He holds up his hands and shakes them at me.

I chuckle. I don't know whose idea it was to give these damn Selells such sexual power over us. I thought we were supposed to work together to save the universes, not fuck.

I put my gaze back on the environment. What I see brings me to one conclusion: the Ugu Mag sure have it good. Humongous foliage pods in the shape of three-leafed clovers rise out of a vast lake. "The first people" lie out on these pods. Some have half of their bodies submerged in the water and the other half resting on top of the pod. These people are gathered in groups and are leisurely socializing. I see a group of children using what looks like a cannon shoot the colored cloth in the air. They're giggling and jumping around on that pod, seemingly having a lot of fun. On the pod in the dead center of the pond, a number of musicians are playing harps, cellos, and violins. It's beautiful music—enough to make me *almost* wish Telman was romantic enough to take me in his arms and spin me a few times.

Far off on the grassy land that lines the lake are fire pits. That's where the food is. And, yes, the Ugu Mag are baring it all—breasts, penises, bushes, and asses. So are we, except I don't have a bush. None of the females of my race do—I guess to make it easier for vampires to access us.

"I say we start here and end up back there," he says, pointing his chin toward the fire pits.

"After me." I dive into the water without delay.

I feel Telman beside me as I seek out the pod with the most bodies dangling from it. Once we find it, I swim to one side and Telman goes to the other side. We like to invade groups of socializing humans as if we are strangers. It makes it all the more interesting, especially on Earth. It's so damn funny to watch chicks competing for Telman's attention. He only craves me, and they're forced to watch him nearly eat me alive with his eyes the entire time. Poor girls.

But the Ugu Mag women we've joined hardly notice him, and the men don't gawk at me in the way Earth men do. What's even more interesting is that our invasion into their circle doesn't seem to make any of them uncomfortable. They move over and make room for us.

"*Ocum, luzk, cumpon, oeyoz bo lumom,*" says a female with a shaved head and skin as white as a marshmallow.

I know their language. Sometimes my father combines it with Enuian. Telman lifts his eyebrows at me because he recognizes it too. She just said,

"The chords are high tenor, and they sound like sex."

"*The 2y, xz, eregop*," replies a male, the stark opposite of the girl in appearance. His skin is as dark as charcoal, and his wooly black hair is longer than mine.

"I hear it," another says. "The tones of infinity."

"How did you get that scar on your face?" a girl with freckled shoulders asks. She's staring at my cheek, rotating her head to view my mark at different angles.

I run a finger down the depression. I always forget it's there until someone points it out. "I underestimated my opponent," I mutter, remembering the fight.

It was a bastillon, a creature of the Moksoar Sea. Its body is long and scaly and its mouth is wide with sharp teeth because it's from the dragon family. What sets it apart from others of its species is that it has twenty sharp claws lining the fins on each side of its body.

Going against my father's wishes, Telman and I tried to pilfer the only pearl link from the black caves the bastillon guards. Needless to say, we failed. I'm fast, but it somehow caught me in its claws and nearly tore me to shreds. I had more than one gash on my face.

That wasn't the first time we chose to defy the great Felix Benel, nor was it the last. However, he picked that opportunity to teach me a lesson. I never knew I was vain until I woke up with the mark on my face. I begged him to make it go away, but he refused. He'd said, "It will heal, Na'ta, when it's ready to heal." That was four hundred Earth years ago. I don't really mind it anymore. There comes a time when we accept what we can't figure out how to change.

The Ugu Mag situated around the pod look confused by what I just said, almost as if they are waiting for me to explain further.

The girl with the freckles narrows her eyes at my chest. "Your breasts are unique. They slope above the sprig. It's attractive."

"Oh." I'm staggered by her comment. I instinctively look at hers. Yes, I see the difference between our breasts. Mine are cone-shaped and plump, and hers are round and plump.

"I agree," Telman says, smirking at me.

She whips her head around to face him. "You are attracted to her?"

"You have no idea," he says in English,

narrowing his eyes at me. He flippantly says something in their language equivalent to "But she's not attracted to me."

"What tongue did you speak?" the male beside me asks Telman.

"English," he answers.

They get that confused look on their faces again.

"It's an ancient language," I chime in.

"There are no ancient languages. We have one language," the female with the freckled shoulders says.

"You are not Ugu Mag, are you?" asks a girl with hair as red as Fawn's.

Usually Telman and I would scram, because we have just exposed ourselves. When he spoke English, he poked the dragon. However, like me, he doesn't believe the Ugu Mag are capable of breathing fire. He and I make eye contact. We are in agreement.

"I'm from Enu; he's from Earth," I reveal. I anticipate where their questions will lead. They will ask what we are, and if I am to remain honest, I'll have to admit that Telman is a Selell.

Most universes are at least a little knowledge-able of vampires. As on the Earth, legends of blood-sucking, night-crawling transmogrified humans exist in other worlds. After hearing a vampire is wading in their pond, they'll probably scatter like frightened dolphins do when a great white shark races into their midst.

"Listen," the male with the long, bushy hair says, inclining his ear toward the sky. "The harmony is spinning past infinity!" He's very excited.

"It has arrived!" another exclaims.

At once, every single one of them emerges from the water and hops onto the pod. The leaf easily bears the weight of them dancing on it. Flabbergasted, Telman and I watch their wet, naked figures.

There's something appealing about the way they move. Their arms glide up high above their heads, and their hands lock with the nearest person. Then they hike up one leg and link it with their neighbor's, then lower it while doing the same with the other leg. It is the most fascinating scene. The ballad chimes one long, harmonious note, and they all bend over and crouch low, waiting for the melody to change.

Telman and I lock eyes and speak without saying a word. I can read his mind. Now he's right in front of me. We stop holding on to the sturdy leaf and let ourselves sink to the bottom of the pond. It's deep, and although we can't hear the beautiful song, he dances me along the floor of the lake. My unromantic vampire has been inspired by the music. He shuffles against the pressure of the water, moving past dangling legs and a few startled deep-water swimmers. This shuffle we're doing doesn't feel corny. His eyes hold me captive. I hear his voice in my head say, *I love you*, and I say it back.

Finally, we emerge, dripping wet, and our feet sink into the spongy grass. We haven't pulled apart. After a moment, he lets go of me to cup my breasts.

"I've wanted to do this ever since that smart Mag chick noticed how magnificent they are." He smirks.

I chuckle, delighting in the moment.

He raises an eyebrow. "Maybe we should return and join Adore and Vestop in the trees."

I'm very tempted. My nipples want to feel the wetness and warmth of his mouth. I want him to take me and ravish me in the way only Telman can. He'll shove me against one of those tree trunks, and we'll break it in half. He'll thrust himself so far inside me that it will feel as though he'll bust through me.

"They're dancing the *wey'lo'lol!*" Adore exclaims.

Telman and I break eye contact and turn to see Adore and Chex standing at the edge of the lake, watching the Ugu Mags' strange dance. Her hair is all tossed up, and she smells and glows like sex.

"Finally," I grumble, but she's not paying me any attention.

Her face is full of light, and she's unable to look away from the Ugu Mag. "Do you mind?" Before any of us can reply, she dives into the water.

We are all gripped by suspense. Telman, Chex, and I can't take our eyes off how her long, lean limbs gracefully carry her across the water. She is an expert swimmer. With her last stroke, she propels herself out of the water and onto the pod, flinging her arms and hiking up her leg in step with the others. She's giggling and engaging with the natives. Adore can find a good time anywhere and with anyone. She is the light. It dawns on me that she's the reason I feel so damn different: better—and I'll admit—happier.

I see that Ugu Mag are roasting vegetables on the fire pits built of stacked wood. There is corn, eggplant, potatoes, and white and yellow squash.

But I'm not hungry for food, and I won't be until my body expends a certain amount of energy.

I notice that the sun is past noon. I feel almost as though we're *not* trying to recover the Scepter of Gant. It's funny how life progresses. One moment I'm being held captive by a thirsty tree, the next I'm getting pummeled by vampires while trying to save my love from being drained by blood slugs, and the next I'm watching a sister—who swore she'd never leave Enu—hop around with the locals in Dag.

"Telman?" I purr. I sound like a stranger; I'm affected by the music and the dancing.

"What is it?" He's perplexed by my alluring tone.

"How about we go into the trees now?" I whisper, already gripped by desperation.

His answer is to slam my back into the rough bark of a tree, just like in my fantasy. He thrusts inside me. My nipple is in his mouth, and he's sucking on it so hard that it aches.

"Bite me!" I scream.

He sinks his teeth into my neck and slams me against the grass, pounding me harder. This is how I've always liked it, but something is amiss. He's so near yet so far away. My body is singing, but my soul is parched.

"Telman," I whimper. I'm trying to keep the tears from rolling out of my eyes.

His fangs retract, and he's motionless on top of me. "What's wrong? Am I hurting you?" He kisses my forehead gently.

I crave more of that. "No."

Now he's even more perplexed.

"Make love to me?" I ask.

Our gray eyes catch each other's gaze.

"Are you sure?" he asks.

I nod, so very sure about it. His hardness smooths itself in and out of me. It feels so damn good that I whimper under the weight of his body. It's all inside me, the emotions of being so close to him that I don't want to exist outside his skin. Our kissing is soft and hot. His mouth always tastes like mint leaves and sweet citrus.

When I run my tongue along his fangs, he throws his head back and bellows a growl that shakes the leaves. My arms wrap around his neck, determined to hold on tight. I can actually feel my orgasm sprouting as I pulsate around him.

"Shit, Navi," he grunts.

"Shit, Telman," I moan.

I don't even recognize the sounds I'm making, but the notes are sharp and grounded at the base of my throat. This is the longest, most intense orgasm I have ever experienced. When I finally let go of the tension in my body, I hear the tail end of Telman's restrained growl. He shouts when it's over, and he collapses on top of me like a rag doll.

We lay silent and still for a long time. I feel him filling me up, and I'm still contracting around him. Our bodies don't want to stop, but we're blown away by what we've just experienced. From the very first time Telman and I had sex, it has been rough. Although he was involved with Gia Scoralini back then, we couldn't resist each other any longer. When it finally happened, it was explosive.

"Why haven't we done this before?" he asks humorously.

We both laugh.

"Because we're impatient."

"You're impatient," he accuses, "not me."

"No way. You are too," I tease.

He lifts his face to look into mine. His expression is sincere. "Baby, I've wanted to give it to you like this for a long time but"—he shrugs—"I go the way you lead me."

"And I go the way you lead me," I say.

"How do you like where I'm leading you now?"

Telman slips in and out of me so slow, so deep that I think I'll burst from the insane sensations.

"Ah…" is all I'm able to moan, but I'm sure he got the gist of it, because he doesn't stop.

Round two…

Adore

IN MY MIND, I AM HOME AND DANCING AMONG friends, except instead of Enuians, they are human. How do they know our dance? Our forearms clap against each other, and our calves knock. The sound they make is melodic. My head is spinning with happiness. I could do this for eternity. Then I happen to catch a glimpse of Chex in the far distance, watching me.

My feet halt and arms drop as I stand still to observe him. I've never stopped dancing until the song comes to an end, but like much of what I've recently experienced, there's always a first time.

"You cannot stop!" a youthful man jubilantly says. His large hands take me by the waist and guide me into his hollow body.

I flinch because I'm shocked. He spoke

Agocum, the first language my father ever taught me.

"He should take his hands off you before I break them," Chex says in my ear. He's pressed against my backside and squeezing me possessively.

But the male has already let go. He's dancing the wey'lo'lol with another partner. I wriggle out of Chex's grasp and drop into the water. I spin around to face him and motion for him to join me. After a moment of confusion, he does. I spring toward him, finally feeling comfortable in my skin. Our chests touch.

"Follow me," I say with my lips close to his.

Before he can kiss me, I swim away and he trails behind me. I swim away from the clovers and keep going until the music fades and there are no humans in sight. Finally Chex overtakes me and swims me to the nearest grassy bank, where we lay dripping wet. I roll out of his arms onto my back. He stretches out alongside me, smoothing the hair from my face.

The sky has traces of orange streaked across it. It's a subtle reminder that this is not Enu. Here, time advances. The sun will move on, the moon will glisten, and we will leave for Ol. Thinking about it makes me shiver.

"Are you cold?" Chex asks and rubs my arm.

I was turning chilly before his hand made contact with my skin, but now I'm warm. "No," I say with a relaxed sigh.

"Then what's going on?"

I flip onto my side and prop myself up to face him. "We're going into Ol, and I'm a little squeamish."

"Don't be, baby. I'll be with you the whole time. All you have to do is walk forward. I won't let anything touch you. I promise." There's a sincere glint in his eyes.

I believe him. Suddenly I remember something. "Your eyes." I smooth a finger across his eyebrows. "They're black, but that's not their real color."

He frowns. I know he's wondering how I know this.

"I could see what was not real about you after I filled you with the light."

Chex rolls onto his back. After a long pause, he puts a finger into each of his eyes. When he's done, there are little black circles on his fingertips. He rubs them together, and they fall like granules into the grass.

I inhale, shocked. He has emerald eyes like mine.

"Another thing," he says. "Earlier, I pretended not to know that I was once called Vestop Mallotnis."

"I don't understand," I confess.

"I have a lot of enemies." He points at his eyes. "These are memorable, and I don't want to be remembered." His green eyes watch me. He looks very different but still the same. "What are you thinking?" He squints as if he's trying to interpret the expression on my face.

"I'm thinking that you look slightly different, but I still recognize you."

"You're not upset that I didn't tell you the truth?" he asks.

"No, I understand."

He lifts his mouth to mine, and his tongue tastes sweet. "I knew you would." He smiles then regards me shrewdly. "You're keen, you know? If you've been swimming, dancing, and playing for... How old are you again?"

"In Earth years?"

He chuckles a little, amused at my newness, I presume. "Yes."

"Eight thousand years."

He lets out a strange whistle. "You're an old lady," he jokes. "On Earth, you'd be a mummy."

"Aren't mummies dead?" I ask.

"Aha!" His voice is pleasant to my ears. "She knows about mummies. Of course, they're real, right?"

"Yes," I say with assuredness. "Certain Earth cultures practiced preserving the body after death—"

Chex kisses me before I can finish. He guides me onto my back and mounts me. Our kissing makes me giddy inside. He is hard against me, but he doesn't spread my legs to slip inside me. Instead, we roll on the grass. Our legs intertwine, and our hands grab at each other's bodies.

"Sorry about that," he whispers, pinning his forehead against my chest. "I'm trying to practice restraint, but I crave you constantly."

"That's very noble of you to act against your impulses."

He lifts his face. He's grinning, amused again. "Are you trying to make this difficult?"

"No!" I say sincerely.

"Ah, shit," he mumbles, losing the battle against his will. He spreads my legs, and he's inside me—again.

CHAPTER 12

THE STEAL

ADORE

After taking a shower, I dress myself. Chex decided to give self-restraint another go and keep his distance, so he suggested that we shower alone. I must say, I rather enjoy this shower contraption. The warm water slithering down my limbs is quite refreshing after our long day. My skin has changed since leaving Enu; grime clings easily to me. My humanity has strengthened.

I clothe myself in the same ensemble I wore earlier—blue pants, shirt, and boots—and once I'm finished, I head to the portal to join the others. Na'ta is wearing similar clothing, except in black. This is the first time I've seen Chex since he gave me space to prepare for the next leg of our journey. He's gazing at me as if he wants to strip my clothes off again. When I smile at him, he turns away and tries to focus on Na'ta and Telman.

"Ready?" he asks them.

"Born ready." Na'ta can hardly contain her enthusiasm.

The portal is lit for us.

"Wait. Do you have the medallion?" she asks me.

I feel for it in my pants pockets. "I have it."

With that confirmed, we hurry through the portal to meet Magnificent Star in the hub. The wire tentacles are already attached to her head, and Tetra is visible in the great beyond.

"The Olligark have prepared to make a stand along their southeastern borders," she says as soon as she's aware of our presence. She narrows her eyes. "I find this odd. The Tarantula is in the northeast, five hundred and thirty-three krugs away—approximately the same as thirteen hundred miles."

"So that makes it easy for us?" Chex asks, regarding her keenly.

"Yes."

"And that didn't happen by mistake?" he further asks.

"I would say—no."

Each of us searches the others' expressions. I

believe one name prevails in all of our thoughts. I consider our histories with this individual. Every face I see—except Magnificent Star's—appears to have a plan for Lario Exgesis, including me. Like me, none of them is willing to disclose their plots.

"It doesn't matter," Telman says with a dismissive shrug. "We do what we have to do, and more if need be." He turns to Na'ta for affirmation. By the look in her eyes, he receives it.

"Now what?" Na'ta asks Magnificent Star.

Magnificent Star walks to the podium and moves her finger around the glass screen. She points out toward Tetra. "See the tiny streak in the sky?" The tip of her finger indicates a small black slit in the muggy sky. It's situated beneath Earth's sun. "That's the portal. You will enter Ol through it."

"And Gia Scoralini and the earth's sun will follow us," I mutter, pondering aloud because we have a problem. "What will be the one factor Lario Exgesis did not anticipate?" I ask Magnificent Star.

A slow smile forms on her face. "He did not anticipate the sun returning to Earth."

We are all relieved to hear that we may have an advantage over him. Now his plan is more lucid. That's why he convinced the Olligark to prepare for attack so far away from where we'll be.

"Once in Ol, you'll see the Tarantula. It's a massive structure, but the Scepter of Gant has a glare that can be seen from afar by those with the eyes of light. There are four such people: Felix Benel, Adore, Chex—"

"Me?" Chex asks very shocked.

"The curse has left you."

He presses his lips together. I know him well enough now to recognize that this is his signal that no further discussion is desired. Chex loathes that he was once victimized by another force. It's more than likely that he's planning retribution.

"And the fourth is Exgesis," Chex says icily.

Magnificent Star nods. "You'll see the glare as soon as you are inside the Tarantula—follow it."

It's time.

Na'ta holds me from behind, and Telman does the same to Chex. The mere power of light is a defiance of space and time. I never see our path, but we are at the foot of the Tarantula. It's true. This construct is fashioned from bones. It's an evil concept, and it's fitting for a place with creatures that thrive in a lightless environment. Ol is supposed to be dark, but the sun that followed us exposes a vast number of odd-shaped structures throughout the sandy terrain that is littered by loose, dry, and bloodied bones.

"Open it," Na'ta tells me. She's restless.

I am too. This universe chills my soul. I call the light to my eyes, and I see the slot that's sized just right for the medallion. I slide the object out of my pocket and into the keyhole, turn it, take it out, and stuff it back into my pocket for safekeeping. Chex must have noticed how my hands shook because he holds one of mine. I can hardly bear the energy here. It's squeezing me and is heavy on my shoulders.

We all wait with bated breath, wondering what will happen next. We do not have to wait long. The Tarantula rises on eight legs, revealing a dark entrance within the leg where I put the key.

"Do you hear that?" Na'ta asks, gazing into the dark hole.

"I do," I whisper. The sound is similar to that of a strong waterfall crashing against the rocks beneath it.

Chex kisses the back of my hand. "Like I said, keep moving forward and I'll cover you, understand?"

I nod. I feel as though my head is bobbing frantically.

"Take the front, Chex. We got the back," Telman says.

Chex glances at me before he leaps into the Tarantula's leg, still holding my hand while making sure I remain behind him. Once we're completely inside, he lets go of my hand.

"See it?" he shouts over his shoulder, above the loud and constant crashing noise. It almost sounds as if the Mtknv are in the vicinity, but the reverberation is too violent to be them.

"Yes!" I see the circular beam of light as I enter the center of the long hallway. It's as if the rays stab through the heart of darkness.

My feet still have not hit the surface, but I move with the speed of the wind up the corridor. The closer I get, the more I can hear them in front, behind, above, and below us. The Olligark are in here. That noise comes from their bones smashing against the floor. I keep advancing because that is what I'm supposed to do. I'm not supposed to fight, but how will I avoid battle? I call the light to my fingers just in case. Oh, how putrid the air is! There is more than the scent of death in it. It holds a sharp, gaseous substance that makes me cough and choke, forcing me to my knees.

Don't breathe, Na'ta cautions me.

I stop inhaling, and when the fogginess fades, I notice that Chex has already swiped me up. He is moving forward, carrying me easily with one arm.

I shake his shoulder, and when he turns to face me, I mouth, "I'm fine."

He sets me back down on my feet without debate.

We are all stunned by what we see next. The floor vibrates with the steps of an Olligark who moves into full view at the end of the hallway behind us. It and we are frozen in a moment of scrutiny. The creature is ten times larger up close. We are merely seeds, and it's an aged tree.

"Give us light!" Na'ta demands.

I grab her and Telman by the forearms and inject them both with a hefty dose of the i'lek'u.

"Now go get the scepter, Adore," she shouts as the creature stomps toward us.

My feet remain planted. The idea of leaving my sister to face this goliath of a being makes me ill. I simply cannot do it.

"Go!" she shouts as it gets closer.

The creature is not quick, but it is powerful. I still have no intentions of leaving her, regardless of what she says or how loud she says it. But Chex yanks my arm, leading me forward.

"Stop! Let go of me!" I strain and struggle against his grasp, halting our progress.

He takes me sternly by the shoulders. "Ad'ru!"

I'm looking into his eyes, but it's hard to focus.

"The longer we stay here, the more dangerous it gets," he shouts. "You do your job. She does her job. The quicker we get the hell out of here!"

I'm antsy, torn between my natural proclivity to protect Na'ta and my obligation to part from her to get what we came for. But he's right. I'm thankful he reminded me of what's important, so I kiss his lips very quickly. I turn toward the glare of the scepter and run as fast as I can.

The pervading blackness still unsettles me, so I spray light out of my fingertips. The two energies battle: my light against Ol's darkness. What's created is a dim gray glow. We arrive at a point where the hallway splits in two directions. The scepter leads me down one way, but two Olligark creatures are stomping their massive bodies toward us from the opposite direction.

Chex doesn't need to tell me to continue running. I keep moving, but he is no longer in front of me. He is behind me, throwing weapons at the creatures. Their deafening hisses grow louder. The sound is so piercing I have to squeeze my hands against my ears. When I turn to see how far away from Chex I have gotten, I can't see him or anything else. The light has been defeated; all that's left is the victorious darkness.

As I turn to gaze forward, I smack right into a wall of bones. I hit it so hard that I'm thrown backward, and I only stop when I crash onto the floor. My head is spinning. I'm slightly dazed but not so much that I can't see that I slammed into the chest of an Olligark. It is coming for me. I want to gasp, but I have to remind myself not to breathe. The sockets of its eyes are fixed on me, and although its skeletal face has no expression, the creature is clearly angry about finding me here.

I'm too far ahead to allow fear to be my demise. I shake off the wooziness, stand, aim my palm at the creature's head, and unleash the light. Its head jerks on impact. My power is strong enough to slow it down, but it doesn't stop coming for me. I aim my other palm at its chest, where the heart of any creature lives. The light blasts another hole in it, and it wobbles and convulses until it crashes and explodes into bone dust.

I'm stunned, hardly able to believe I, Ad'ru, just killed such a stalwart being with the power of light.

But just when I think I'm out of immediate danger, here comes another, and another. Two of them!

I'm outnumbered, but there is no time to sulk about it. I repeat what I have just done. I shoot the light into the head and heart of one of them. As it convulses, the other one advances close enough to raise its arms above me. My heart sinks. It means to crush me. But it jerks backward once, then twice, until it topples over and hits the floor so hard the Tarantula shakes beneath my feet.

I take comfort in the familiarity of the body pressing against my backside.

Chex asks desperately, "Are you okay?" I nod. He kisses the side of my face and turns me around to face him. "Listen, baby, we're faster. We see any more of those assholes, we don't fight. We just run right past them. Got it? Because the fighting is slowing us down, and I think that's what they're here to do."

I nod again. We enfold our fingers and hold tightly to each other's hands before we dart off. I stay by his side as we turn down more corners and dash by more creatures. I feel as though it's taking forever to reach the Scepter of Gant, but it's near. The light turns brighter the closer we get to it.

And then we come to an abrupt stop. Five Olligark creatures guard a wide entrance, and behind them, I see it. The Scepter of Gant is a long rod that's suspended in midair. The guards do not budge. Instead, they watch us, a challenge in their hollow eyes.

"We're here!" Na'ta shouts as she stops beside me.

Telman is on the other side of Chex. I'm gripped by relief. They're safe.

It takes the sight of all four of us to cajole the Olligark from their posts. They shift forward, advancing like one stealthy unit. If I weren't so determined to reach the scepter, I would be very intimidated. I feel Chex's hand against my lower back.

"See the one in the middle? Slip right between his legs," he instructs me.

I focus on the triangular-size space between the Olligark's sinewy knees, which lines up with the lit scepter beyond the threshold of the opening.

"There's about fifty more on our ass!" Telman shouts, stabbing a thumb over his shoulder. "The sun must've already passed on or something!"

That's all Chex needs to hear. He tosses six of the metal balls Na'ta gave him, and instead of staying to see what happens when the balls make contact, I shoot toward the triangular space.

"Ad'ru!" Na'ta shrieks with fear.

She doesn't know our plan, but it's too late to soothe her worry. I'm inside the enormous, dark cubicle. This is strange. I can't hear any of the fighting taking place beyond the threshold. I welcome the silence, but I know that I must do this quickly. I make haste toward the long metal rod. The first thing I notice is that there's nothing fascinating about the Scepter of Gant. I thought it would be adorned with diamonds or rubies or pearls, but no.

Before I can reach it, I'm stopped by two strong arms wrapping around me. My head is foggy, and I try to comprehend the fact that I'm being moved away from my destination. The body against me infuses me with warmth.

"Lario Exgesis," I say in a strained voice as I try to wriggle out of his grasp.

He squeezes me tighter and throws me on the floor. Once I'm down, he grabs my wrists and lays himself on top of me. His knees squeeze my legs together so that I cannot move.

"I can smell him all over you," he hisses like a serpent. He smashes his lips against mine, trying to force me to kiss him.

I turn my face. "Get off me!"

"Lost my advantage, I see," he says, wearing a sinister grin. "That's too bad, because I want you and I'm going to have you."

It dawns on me that the more I struggle, the more turned on he becomes. He's hard against me.

"What do you want?" I ask in a contained, calm voice.

Lario Exgesis hesitates. "I want you to get up and take that scepter off the stump for *us*."

"What do you mean, for us?" I snap.

"You and me. I'm your bond, not that sewer dweller Chex. You want powerful? You want to rule the universes beside a king? Then take that scepter and choose me." His lips almost graze mine as he whispers, "I want you, Ad'ru."

"You said that already," I say spitefully. His ambitions have angered me. "I can never love you, Selell. You are too evil."

His eyes expand. He looks insane before he smashes his lips against mine and forces his tongue in my mouth. His mouth refuses to release mine, and I'm forced to kiss him until he stops.

"None of your folks will survive, not Fawn or

Clarity or *Chex*," he growls. "You want to know why?"

My eyes narrow to slits, and my lips clamp together tightly. I will not let him kiss me again.

His eyes blaze with insanity. "Because the Olligark are coming!" He pushes his man part against my groin. "And so am I." He snickers. What a wicked sound he makes.

We are both distracted by sparks of light hitting the room's entrance. Chex is throwing himself against an invisible shield that keeps him out. The light that sparks upon impact reveals his tortured face. Lario Exgesis looks even more pleased with himself. I must act.

The Selell gazes down at me, and before he can say another word, I press my lips to his. We're kissing, and he's too consumed by me to realize what I'm doing. I pull the i'lek'u from the depths of my belly and shove it into his mouth. It's not just any light—it's the light of recovery. Lario Exgesis rolls off of me to curl into a tight ball. The light pains him because it's attacking.

Adore! Where are you? a desperate voice says in my consciousness.

I leap to my feet and race toward the Scepter of Gant. "Cl'auta!" I call as I grasp the rod.

She appears on the opposite side of me. I'm extremely relieved to see her. She has encased me, and she's not alone. The Selell Baron Ze Feldis now stands beside her. They glare at Lario Exgesis, who's scooting toward us, still fighting the agony.

"Are you on Earth?" I ask her.

"Yes, we are, but where are we now?" Cl'auta looks terribly confused.

"This is Ol. Has the sun returned to Earth?" I ask in a rush.

"Yes, it has."

I'm gripped by a grave feeling. The floor shakes violently under my feet. I lift off the ground. I am still unable to hear any sound outside this room, but I can see Na'ta, Telman, and even Chex still fighting.

"The dark has fallen again. We'll never make it out of here without your help. Pan'a'tua, is she still with you?" I ask.

Cl'auta takes my shoulders, looks deep into my eyes, and says, "Show me what you need."

I STAND ON THE SURFACE OF SHIMMERING, CLEAR water. It's a tranquil sea that stretches into infinity.

There are no mountains or valleys or forests in sight. The scepter is still in my hands. Clarity did exactly as I asked.

Lario Exgesis is here with me. Telman, Na'ta, and Chex are on Earth with her. I must do this without them. Na'ta wants the Scepter of Gant for herself. Even if it should be in the hands of the daughters of Benel, it must be given to us by the rightful owner, and that is the Mtknv.

Lario Exgesis is woozy as he stands. His eyes shift from the scepter to my face. He looks as if he's on the verge of striking me until, all of a sudden, he tenses. "What have you done to me?"

"I have broken our bond."

His hands fly up to squeeze his head, and he shuts his eyes tight. "Where is it?" he asks when he opens his eyes.

"I've taken the light away from you."

He leaps toward me, but my palm is already lifted. I douse him with the light. Lario Exgesis slumps over and drops on top of the water as the liquid stirs under us. The Mtknv are rising, molding themselves into form.

An uncountable number of liquid creatures surround us. Ktkl has taken a position between Lario Exgesis and me. His huge eyes fall over the scepter in my hand. He pulls his eyebrows together while belting out a loud sound of crashing waves.

Another Mtknv creature takes form on the opposite side of him. Her clear bare breasts and wavy watery hair distinguish her from the males. Unlike Ktkl, who is girded in a shendyt skirt that grazes his knees, her skirt is long and hides her feet. But like Ktkl, she's peering at the Scepter of Gant in my hand.

"This is not the agreement," Ktkl says to me.

"But it was stolen from you by him," I say, glancing at Lario Exgesis.

"It was," he concurs.

"Isn't it the reason he has to stand trial?" I ask.

The female lets out a loud sound. She's communicating with Ktkl, and he is listening. He says something back to her in their language, which appears to anger her. She sets her enraged eyes on Lario Exgesis.

"He cannot stand trial now," Ktkl says as if he's accusing me of wrongfully changing Lario Exgesis's fate. "The elder cannot pronounce judgment on the vampire because you have atoned for his crime by returning the Scepter of Gant."

"What if I keep it?" I ask. My father did say that it must remain with us, but Father must know that I could never take it without permission. Na'ta may be a pilferer, but I am certainly not.

The female elder, who understands what I've just said, bellows out another series of noises.

"You are the lifeblood," he says, repeating her words. "Our fates are intertwined." He gazes at the object in my hand. "If you ask for it, then we must give it."

"What if I had stolen it?" I ask to satisfy my curiosity and confirm that I have done what was intended for me to do.

"May I?" Ktkl asks, holding out his hand to receive the scepter.

I give it to him without hesitation. He hands it to the elder.

"Open your mouth," he says to me.

Like before, I lift my chin and open my mouth. The elder puts her finger on my tongue. When she removes her finger, she displays the tiny drop of water that Ktkl once put inside me. She smashes it on the end of the long plain rod that is the Scepter of Gant.

"If you had not returned it to us," Ktkl says, "then it would have remained locked. But now…"

The metal casing falls off the scepter, and when it hits the water, it disintegrates with a splash. Even Lario Exgesis's eyes grow wide at the sight of the glass rod with lit gold, red, purple, and green flakes floating inside it. There are also solid gold knobs at each end of the scepter. It seems Exgesis didn't know that the scepter was locked.

As Ktkl holds the scepter out for me to take, I'm knocked off my feet and hit impenetrable water. I see the back of a woman with long black hair streaking up and away. She has snatched the scepter out of Ktkl's hand.

The rain is falling. The Mtknv are in an uproar. Lario Exgesis is gone. It is as if the world is spinning out of control.

Then I see the back of the thief speeding toward us. My heart drops when I see Chex has one hand clasped around her neck. I'm back on my feet, and water splashes me as he slams her against the surface and tears the rod from her grasp.

"Take it, Ad'ru," he says gruffly as he holds up the rod.

I rush over to take it from him. Then his free hand slips into his jacket and comes out clenching a dagger.

"Chex, no!" I shout, but it's too late.

His arm swipes across his chest to slice off her

head, but his blade is stopped by the solid block of water surrounding the woman.

Ktkl's broad hands take Chex by the wrist. "Murder is not allowed in Mtknv. If you kill, you will be judged and sentenced."

I'm relieved that Ktkl stopped him from killing the female Selell! I am also dreading the ire behind Chex's expression.

In one agile move, he leaps to his feet and glares at the petrified Selell, who I assume is Gia Scoralini. "If you want to save her life, then you better make sure I don't get hold of her outside your borders."

I study the frozen face of Gia Scoralini. Her eyes are bulging. Chex has definitely frightened her. She is an attractive creature who resembles Na'ta.

"What happens outside Mtknv is not our concern," Ktkl replies.

Chex turns his angry eyes on me. "What the hell was that, Ad'ru? You came here without me!"

I drop my face to look at my feet. I knew he would be very upset when I saw him again.

But his finger on my chin lifts my face. "Don't ever do that again?"

"I will not," I promise him.

His tender lips kiss mine. It's a very quick kiss.

He wraps an arm around my waist and asks Ktkl, "Can we leave?"

"You are free to go," Ktkl answers.

I bow my head to my Mtknv friend, and he touches my forehead with one of his enormous fingers. A cool liquid sensation trickles down my throat.

"When you call, the Mtknv will come," he declares.

The water creatures remain true to form, being the first to make an exit. With a thunderous splashing sound, they melt into the sea, taking Gia Scoralini with them.

Chex and I are alone, and for a moment, I consider the beautiful sun that hangs above Mtknv and the soft breeze that flows up my nostrils. I hope it will stop my head from spinning and my legs from dropping out from under me. All around me has just turned...

EPILOGUE

ADORE

I open my eyes. My lids and my limbs are heavy. I'm lying on my side, and my head is resting on something familiar. I gaze up, blinking to focus my eyes.

Chex plants a soft kiss on my lips. "You woke up."

His gentle whisper soothes me, but I cannot ignore Na'ta, Cl'auta, Falu, Pan'a'tua, and the two sisters I have never laid eyes on, Glo and Zillael, hovering around my bed.

"All right, you can leave now," Na'ta says snobbishly to Chex.

He grunts harshly in her direction and then kisses me softly on my forehead. "I'll be back." He doesn't give Na'ta a second look before strolling gracefully through an opening.

It dawns on me why I lost consciousness: Pan'a'tua used the power of matter on me. My sisters and I have adverse reactions to it. It takes more time for our bodies to reconstruct after they have been deconstructed.

"Oh my God, Ad'ru!" Fawn nearly cries as she hurries to squeeze me tight. "We've been looking for you. Hoping to find you!" She holds me as if her life depends on it.

"I'm fine," I assure her as I rake my fingers through her soft hair. Once she lets go of me, Cl'auta hugs me.

"It's been a nightmare," Cl'auta says, shuddering as she recalls what she has experienced.

I look at Pan'a'tua, who's standing at the foot of the bed. She smiles at me, which is her equivalent to a hug.

I smile back. "How are you, Pan'a'tua?"

"*Tek sek' a,*" she says, still grinning. *I'm in hell.*

She's said that many times regarding the earth. I smile at her and extend my arms. She takes my hand, and after I inject her with the i'lek'u, the light of home, she lets out an indulgent sigh.

"You put one over on me," Na'ta says, smirking.

Her arms are crossed, and she looks as brash as ever.

"I had to, Na'ta. I knew you had your own ambitions."

"Damn right." She winks at me. "Score one for you, Adore. You're good at this shit."

Cl'auta throws her a quick glance. I can see that she's become a little acquainted with Na'ta and is bothered by her insolence. One of my sisters chuckles quietly at Cl'auta's reaction.

"Zillael," I say, identifying her by the yellow eyes and dark hair. She had these traits as an infant.

She turns silent, and her eyes nervously expand. "Yes?"

Those eyes—I thought I'd never see them again. When she was first born, I thought she was the most beautiful creature I'd ever seen because of her eyes. They are the color of diamonds and the rusek'nelek leaf.

"Glo…" There's a harmonic ring in my voice.

She gulps. "That's me."

"Your eyes are still beautiful," I whisper.

"So are yours," she replies.

We smile at each other. Cl'auta and Falu sit on the bed and rub my bare legs. It's their turn to comfort me in this manner. The first time we sat like this, Cl'auta had been wounded by a Selell. The second time, Falu had been poisoned by Lario Exgesis. And that's when I remember…

"I was bonded to the Selell Exgesis," I tell Falu.

"I know. We figured it out," she says.

"We have a lot of work ahead of us, Ad'ru," Cl'auta says. "Are you staying here? Are we now seven sisters?" The glint of hope makes her eyes sparkle.

"I have to. I'm in love," I confess, unable to restrain my sheepish grin.

Of course Na'ta grunts bitterly, followed by a forceful sigh.

"You don't approve?" my ever-so-serious Cl'auta asks, turning to her.

Na'ta furrows her eyebrows as if she didn't expect such a question. "He's okay." She shrugs. "He likes to fight, but so do I."

Cl'auta squints at her, assessing her before turning back to me with a smile. "He's waiting for you. He's very impatient."

"That's because he wants to fuck her into oblivion," Na'ta mutters under her breath.

This time, both Cl'auta and Falu shoot her a look. Then they look at each other, and Cl'auta smiles weakly. I'm sure Falu just told her something about Na'ta. Falu and Na'ta are acquainted but have never been very close.

"We should leave him to you," Cl'auta says with an exaggerated whisper, remaining calm even though Na'ta has flustered her.

Na'ta glares at Cl'auta because she realizes that, unlike herself, Cl'auta was born to lead, and lead she will. One by one, my sisters file out of the room. Na'ta is the last. Before she goes, she rushes back to me and throws her arms around me. We squeeze each other tightly.

"We made it out of there," she whispers.

"We did."

"We couldn't hold them off any longer."

"I'm so sorry, Na'ta."

"No, don't be. We're safe now. I love you, sister." She kisses my cheek.

"I love you too, Na'ta." I kiss hers.

She sniffs and wipes the wetness from her cheeks. She was crying? Na'ta has always been Enuian in that she never cries.

As soon as she's gone, Chex rushes into the room. Na'ta was right. Without saying a word, he ceremoniously unwraps the clothes from my body and commences to, as she said, fuck me into oblivion.